Cobra Strike

Patrick E. Thomas

iUniverse, Inc.
Bloomington

Cobra Strike

iUniverse books may be ordered through booksellers or by contacting:

iUniverse
1663 Liberty Drive
Bloomington, IN 47403
www.iuniverse.com
1-800-Authors (1-800-288-4677)

ISBN: 978-1-4759-4383-2 (sc)
ISBN: 978-1-4759-4384-9 (hc)
ISBN: 978-1-4759-4385-6 (e)

Library of Congress Control Number: 2012914445

Printed in the United States of America

iUniverse rev. date: 8/23/2012

Chapter 1

The night was pitch black as the two stealth Raven helicopters approached the targeted landing zone at the border of Pakistan and Iran. The Ravens were the latest in advanced technology rotor craft. They could cruise at Mach .8 and had a range of 2,000 miles. The skins on the Ravens were radar-impregnable and could withstand a direct hit from an RPG suffering no damage whatsoever. They were heavily armed. They carried four Hellfire air to surface missiles and six air-to-air AIM-9X Sidewinder heat seeking missiles. They also had mounted in recessed compartments two 50 caliber Gatling guns. These two Ravens had launched from the USS Enterprise in the Gulf of Persia about two hours before. Each Raven had a cargo of six US Navy SEALs aboard. This was the famous SEAL Team 6, the same SEAL Team that killed Osama bin Laden about two years before. They were led by Captain Zakkova Ikanovich. Zakkova was an extraordinary specimen. He stood 6'8" and weighed 350 pounds of solid muscle. People would stare at him like he was some type of god because his was so big and incredibly handsome. Their mission tonight was to locate and terminate Ayman al-Zawahiri, the new leader of Al Qaida after Osama bin Laden was killed by this same team of SEALs about two years ago. HUMINT (human intelligence) had revealed that al-Zawahiri was sheltered in a compound in the Iranian town of Zehedan, which was only fifteen miles from the Pakistani border and the SEAL's landing zone. The Ravens were to land on Pakistani soil right at the border of Iran and Pakistan. The SEALs would have to hump the fifteen miles from the Ravens to Zehedan.

The SEALS in the Ravens scouted around the landing zone, using infrared goggles to make sure no one was near the landing zone. The

Ravens made virtually no noise and the interior lights were set in NVG mode to make them invisible in the dark night air. After assuring themselves that no hostiles were in the area, the Ravens lightly touched down on the landing zone. Captain Ikanovich led his team out of the first Raven and then moved them to the second Raven to meet up with the other six SEALs. The SEALs were all dressed in black with their faces charcoaled to make them indistinguishable in the night sky. They all wore the latest in technology infrared vision goggles. Their goggles, the latest development in night vision, were made by SA Photonics and were called the High Resolution Night Vision System, HRVNS for short. These were infrared thermal imaging goggles that illuminated objects by their heat source in the infrared light spectrum. The light head mounted display offers an 82.5 degree of high-definition vision versus 40 degrees for regular NVGs.

"Mike, you take point and I'll be right behind you. All you other men fall into a single file line and follow Mike and me. Let's move it guys," commanded Zakkova.

"Aye, aye sir, we're ready to march."

The terrain from the landing zone to Zehedan was mostly flat desert so the men chopped up the fifteen miles quickly. Mike, the point man, had a GPS tracker with the coordinates of al-Zawahiri's compound programmed into it. It was just a matter of following the GPS milestones until they came upon the compound.

The SEALs stopped about a mile from the compound, which was sitting on a knoll with no other structures around it. Zakkova did some recon by focusing his generation 3 infrared binoculars on the compound. There was a ten foot wall surrounding the compound, with a main gate manned by four guards.

"Okay men we're going through the front door of this one. Jesse, Dave take out those four guards at the main gate," directed Zakkova.

Jesse and Dave lay down flat on the ground and unfolded their state-of-the-art sniper rifles. Jesse was just over six feet tall and weighed one hundred and ninety pounds of solid muscle. Dave was only about five foot eight but was tightly compacted with bulging muscles. They were M40A1s that were a special sniper rifle developed for the Marine Corp snipers by craftsmen at Quantico Virginia. These guns had a range of 3,000 yards and were equipped with powerful infrared scopes. Both rifles had sound suppressors attached to the muzzles of the guns. The SEALs aimed carefully and fired off two rounds apiece. The bullets struck the four guards in their heads, which showed up in the rifle scopes as pink mists.

After Jesse and Dave had taken out the front gate guards, the SEALs ran to the gate as fast as they could to secure it. When they got there they moved the dead guards' bodies into the guard house and then looked inside to determine how many security cameras were operating and where they were focused. They used their infrared goggles to find out if there were any other guards roaming outside of the compound. They spotted two guards in the front and two guards in the back of the building pacing back and forth over the lush landscaping. These guards would have to be neutralized before the SEALs could enter the building.

"Jerry, Zack take out the guards in the front and back of the building. When you're done signal me with two mike clicks and then station yourselves at the back of the building in case anyone tries to escape. Mike, stay at the guard house and radio me if anyone approaches the compound," said Zakkova.

Zakkova then threw three baseball sized globes onto the lawn in front of the building. These were electronic camera jammers that would make the security cameras freeze on the last frame they were on. These were made by a high tech company called Inverse Technologies who dealt exclusively with the U.S. government. They made sophisticated electronic devices that could do amazing things. They also owned the most powerful super computers in the world that enabled them to hack into any computer system in the world. They fed a constant stream of intel to the NSA and CIA.

When Zakkova got the two mike clicks from Jerry and Zack, he quickly led the nine other SEALs to the front door of the building. The building was three stories high, and they assumed that al-Zawahiri would be in one of the rooms on the third floor. Zakkova opened the door and rolled another camera jammer into the foyer. This disabled the security cameras on the first floor entrance. Zakkova then moved from room to room on the first floor, clearing them of any hostiles. He found one man in the family room watching TV. He snuck up behind him and silently slit his throat with his EK combat knife. The first floor was now cleared.

The inside of the building was opulently decorated. There was a large winding staircase in the middle of the lobby that led to the second and third floors. The SEALs made their way up the staircase to the second floor where Zakkova rolled out another camera jammer. There were six doors on the second floor separating different rooms. They moved to the first door on the right and pressed their infrared goggles on the door to find out how many people were in the room. The goggles showed that there were two people in the room standing close together. Zakkova lightly tapped the door with the muzzle of his silenced HK53 submachine gun. The camera showed one of the persons heading for the door. The other person stayed where he was directly in the path of the doorway. This would make for an easy second kill shot. When the door opened Zakkova gave the man answering the door a double tap to the head with his HK53 killing the man instantly. Zakkova quickly took aim at the second man and gave him a triple tap to the head with his submachine gun.

The SEALs moved to the first door on the left. The infrared goggles showed that the room was unoccupied. Just then Zakkova got a radio call from Mike at the guard house.

"Zakkova, I see an Iranian military vehicle heading our way," said Mike. Mike was a wiry man with lean muscles but he was very strong.

"Take them out. Use the suppressed 50 caliber machine gun. Make sure you get them all. Be careful when you approach the back of the vehicle. Radio me when you're done," ordered Zakkova.

"Aye, aye sir, it will be done."

The military vehicle turned out to be a full two ton covered truck with two men in the front seat. When it got to about one hundred yards from the gate, Mike left the guard house and positioned himself in the middle of the driveway. When the truck got to within twenty-five yards of the guard house Mike let loose with a barrage of 50 caliber rounds from his machine gun. Glass shards from the windshield scattered everywhere. The truck rolled forward a few more feet and then stopped. Mike walked up to the truck and looked inside of the truck cabin. He saw the driver and his passenger shredded to pieces from the 50 caliber rounds. Blood and tissue were pasted all over the cab of the truck. He then went to the back of the truck and carefully opened the flaps of the canvas covering. The truck bed was filled with weapons, AK74s, MP3s, RPGs and hundreds of Glock 17s. Mike went back to the guard house where his back pack was and retrieved two blocks of C4 explosives with remote detonators. He went back to the truck and set the C4 blocks in the bed and activated the remote detonators.

"Zakkova, the vehicle has been neutralized. The back of the truck was filled with weapons. I set it up so we can have some fireworks when we leave," Mike radioed Zakkova.

"Good job, Mike. I can't wait to see what you've come up with. We'll be done here in about ten more minutes."

Meanwhile back in the building, Zakkova and the SEALs kept checking the six rooms on the second floor. They found two young girls inside the second room on the left. They were probably there for al-Zawahiri's pleasures. They cuffed their wrists and ankles and put duct tape over their mouths. The second and third rooms on the right were empty. At the doorway to the third room on the left the infrared goggles showed four people in the room. This had to be the security room. The men inside were probably watching the security monitors for intruders. There were two men seated on the left side of the room and two on the right side.

"Doug, you take out the two on the left side of the room. I'll take care of the ones on the right," says Zakkova. Doug was six feet five and weighed around two hundred and fifty pounds. But he was surprisingly quick for such a big man.

Zakkova tapped the door with the muzzle of his HK53 submachine gun. The first man on the left came to the door

"Who is it and what do you want?" asked the man.

Zakkova responded in perfect unaccented Arabic, "It is Muhammad. I have some important requests from the Emir that I need you to take care of."

When the man opened the door a crack, Zakkova kicked it in with his size fifteen boot. The blow knocked the door off of its hinges and broke the nose of the man who had opened it. Zakkova wasted no time in killing him and the second man on the left with his HK53. Doug quickly stepped in the room and took out the two men seated on the right side of the room. The second floor was now secured and the security station was out of order.

The SEALs moved up to the third floor. There was only one door for the whole floor. Zakkova concluded that the third floor must be al-Zawahiri's suite. The infrared goggles showed four people in the room and one of them was al-Zawahiri. There was one person sitting alone on the left side wall and three others that were grouped together on the other side of the room.

"Okay men this is it. We've got four hostiles in the room. One is al-Zawahiri. We're going to have to break down the door and enter the room and kill everyone but al-Zawahiri. Do not shoot al-Zawahiri. I have something special in mind for him. We'll have the element of surprise so this should not be difficult. Everyone rushes in when I knock down the door. You ready? Let's go," directed Zakkova.

Zakkova knocked down the door by crashing his massive forearm into it. The men rushed into the room and took up positions. Al-Zawahiri was sitting in a big stuffed chair watching child pornography on TV. The other three men were sitting at a table playing cards. The SEALs quickly dispatched the three men at the table by blowing their brains out with their high caliber rounds of ammunition. The SEALs were so fast that the men didn't have time to grab their pistols sitting on the table. Zakkova went immediately to where al-Zawahiri was seated and put him at gun point.

"What's the meaning of this you scoundrels? You will die horrible deaths when my men get to you," shouted al-Zawahiri in perfect English. Al-Zawahiri was a small man with a big belly.

"Sorry Al but your porn party is over. My, my, a devout Muslim such as you watching that trash. I'm sure Allah is taking note of that. By the way your men are pretty much indisposed right now. They won't be coming for us anytime soon. And it appears that your glorious terrorist career is about to come to an end."

"You sorry infidels, how much cash do you want? I can make you all millionaires," pleaded al-Zawahiri.

"We didn't come here to get rich asshole. We came to put the most despicable terrorist pig out of business."

"How dare you call me a pig? You may kill me but there are thousands of brave men and women dedicated to our cause. Someone will replace me and we'll continue our attacks on you kafirs until you and the Zionist dogs are wiped off the face of the earth. Then the Muslims will rule the world under Sharia law," said al-Zawahiri.

"You have big dreams Al but you'll never see that day come. Good will always prevail over evil like all through the ages. You pigs kill women and children. You will surely rot in hell for that."

Zakkova then walked over to al-Zawahiri and removed his glasses.

"What! Give me back my glasses infidel."

"You won't need them where you're going Al."

Zakkova then removed the pack from his back and laid it down on the floor in front of him. He opened it up and removed a one hundred foot one hundred and forty pound red King Cobra.

"I have someone I want you to meet Al. Strike neck Max!"

Max the King Cobra sprung to action immediately and was on al-Zawahiri's lap in a split second. Al-Zawahiri screamed out in fear. He had never seen a snake that large and menacing before. Max rose up to eye level with al-Zawahiri and then spit venom into his eyes that permanently blinded him. Al-Zawahiri screamed out in pain. Next Max struck al-Zawahiri's neck on the left side and tore out his carotid artery with his four-inch needle-sharp fangs. Max then tore out al-Zawahiri's right carotid artery. Al-Zawahiri's blood started gushing out both sides of his neck. He would bleed out and die in less than two minutes.

"David, did you record all of this on the camera?" asked Zakkova.

"Yes, I got it all along with the rest of the mission so far," said David pointing at his camera. David was tasked with filming the raid to prove that the mission was successful.

"Good. Here Max, come here boy for a treat."

Max quickly climbed off al-Zawahiri's lap and crawled over to Zakkova. Zakkova gave Max a big chunk of milk chocolate and Max was in heaven. Chocolate was his favorite food.

"That snake is unbelievable. How did you make him tame and so smart?" asked Bill.

"Oh, Max is a special creature. I love him with all of my heart and he loves me."

Zakkova then put Max back into his bag and slung it over his shoulder. To give an idea how strong Zakkova was, he carried Max who weighed one hundred and forty pounds plus one hundred pounds of gear like the rest of the SEALs did.

"Roger, do you have our calling card ready?" asked Zakkova.

"Yes, Zakkova just let me take it out of my pack."

From his pack Roger removed a pig's head and placed it on al-Zawahiri's lap. This would be the ultimate insult to Muslims because the Quran forbids the eating of pork because it considers the pig to be the vilest of creatures on earth. Muslims kill pigs whenever they see one.

"Okay men, mission accomplished. Let's get out of this shithole," commanded Zakkova. "Dave, make sure we recover all of the camera jammers both inside and outside of the building."

The jammers had transponders on them so they were easy to locate. The SEALs left the building and headed for the gate.

"Jerry, Zack we're done here so meet us at the gate."

When Jerry and Zack came around the front to the gate Zakkova asked Mike to set off his little fireworks display. Once everyone was clear of the truck Mike removed the remote control for the detonators and pushed the button to explode the C4 in the bed of the truck. A huge explosion followed by a big red fireball lit up the dark night sky. It was quite a spectacle.

"Well, if no one knew we were here they do now," said Zakkova.

The SEALs started hiking back to the Ravens with a spring in their step. About five miles from the compound Zakkova heard something.

"Listen, do you hear that. It sounds like helicopters. We must have waked our neighbors up. In fact it sounds like Russian made Kamov K52 helicopters. These are heavily armed and deadly in their own right but still no match for a Raven. I know Iran has some of those in their arsenal. I'd better call the Ravens for support." Zakkova then spoke into his encrypted radio. "Raven 1 and 2 this is nighthawk. We have company coming our way. Sounds like Kamov K52 helicopters. We need air support now. Nighthawk out," said Zakkova.

"Nighthawk we read your position. Hang tight and we'll take out that little problem for you. Raven 1 out."

The Ravens lifted off the landing zone in Pakistan and quickly headed for Zehedan. About two clicks over the border their radars picked up the two Kamov K52 helicopters. Because of the stealth technology built into the Ravens, the Iranian helicopters could not spot them on their radars. The Ravens quickly closed in to the Kamov 52s and lined up their targeting radars. Once the radars beeped and the target light shined green, the Ravens fired two sidewinder missiles apiece each targeted at the two Kamov 52s. The AIM-9X Sidewinders flew at Mach 10. It was a launch and forget missile system. Its infrared radar would lock on to a heat source and track it down and strike it. The Sidewinders immediately found their targets and locked on to them. Each missile struck the Kamov 52s right at the exhaust ducts of the helicopters. There were two large explosions followed by large fireballs when the Sidewinders hit their targets. The Kamov 52s crashed to the earth full of flames.

"Nighthawk this is Raven 1. The airborne threats have been neutralized. We have you on radar. Stay where you are. We will pick you up in about two minutes," said the pilot of Raven 1.

"Roger that Raven 1. We'll be waiting," responded Zakkova.

The whole mission at the compound took only thirty minutes and they had killed Ayman al-Zawahiri, the real brains behind al-Qaida. This would be a real setback for al-Qaida. Al-Zawahiri called all of the shots and arranged for financing for all terrorist attacks around the world. Al-Zawahiri had a big plan to strike the U.S. again but now that would never happen.

The SEALs boarded the Ravens when they landed and were airlifted back to the USS Enterprise in the Persian Gulf.

Chapter 2

"Okay men, let's meet in the Stateroom at 0500 for a debriefing of the mission," said Zakkova.

Before the debriefing the SEALs sat down for a hearty breakfast. Missions like this always left them famished. While they were eating Captain Mewbourne of the USS Enterprise came in to greet them.

"Congratulations men. You have done our country a great service. You should be proud of yourselves because I am certainly proud of you. It's been an honor having you on the USS Enterprise. You will always be welcomed on my ship whenever you need it for your missions. My heartfelt thanks to you all."

The Captain was met with a round of applause from the SEALs and all of the sailors that were in the room.

All of the SEALs mustered at the Stateroom at 0500 hours for the mission debriefing

"Outstanding mission, men, everything went as planned. Every one of you performed flawlessly. Al-Zawahiri had been on the loose commanding al-Qaida since 9/11. We took him out tonight and al-Qaida will be hard pressed to replace him with someone as intelligent as al-Zawahiri was. The world will be much safer because of what you accomplished last night. I will be putting in requests for Silver Stars for all of you for the bravery and valor you displayed on this mission," said Zakkova.

There was a loud round of applause after Zakkova said this. A Silver Star would look good in their jackets and help propel their careers in the US Navy.

"Listen men, I have some news for you that may leave you disheartened. After fifteen glorious and proud years serving as a U.S. Navy SEAL I am retiring. I can't put into words what a pleasure it has been serving with you men. You are the most ferocious warriors on the planet. There is nothing you could do with your lives as honorable as serving your country as a U.S. Navy SEAL. I will deeply miss leading you men into battle. You have all given my life great meaning. You are extraordinary individuals that I love with all of my heart. Even though I'll be retired, you can still come to me at any time for help and advice. I hope you will do that because I am going to miss you terribly. Oh, and I almost forgot, Max wishes you the best and says he is proud that he could serve with you. There will be a ceremony at the White House three days from now and you are all invited to attend. They are going to promote me to Rear Admiral before I retire. Yeah, I know big deal. Also, I will proudly award each of you with a Silver Star at the ceremony so make sure your calendar is clear that day.

All of the SEALs stood up and clapped loudly at Zakkova's announcement. Most of them had tears in their eyes. They loved Zakkova and had loved serving under him. Zakkova was irreplaceable in their eyes so they were all saddened by his announcement.

"Dave, Admiral Harward said we can release the video of the mission. Get it on YouTube immediately. I am sure it will become the most watched video in the world."

Chapter 3

It was a bright sunny June day at the Rose Garden. Assembled there were the most powerful men and women in the US government. The president, the vice president, the Secretary of State, the Director of the CIA, the Director of the NSA, the Director of Homeland Security, and the Navy's CNO and the Chairman of the Joints Chief of Staff. The staffs of these people were also in attendance along with Zakkova's Seal Team. This was in effect a retirement party for Captain Zakkova Ikanovich who would soon become a Rear Admiral in the Navy.

"Ladies and gentlemen I am honored today to be hosting this awards ceremony and retirement party for one of the most valiant warriors in history, Captain Zakkova Ikanovich. The deeds and services this man has performed the last fifteen years are unparalleled. He has fought the good fight and has won all of his battles. The country and the armed forces will deeply miss this honorable man. His acts of courage are too numerous to mention here today and if I did, I would have to kill you all," said the president.

His last comment brought a round of laughter.

"There has been no enemy of this country who has escaped the cunning and treacherous bravery of this man. He has truly been a knight in shining armor for the United States of America. First off, Admiral Harward would like to pin some stars on this great man."

"Yes sir I would. Captain Zakkova Ikanovich I hereby promote you to a Rear Admiral in the US Navy," said Admiral Harward as he pinned three stars on Zakkova's label.

"Thank you sir, I am deeply honored and moved to be awarded these stars," said Zakkova as he gave Admiral Harward a stiff salute.

"Now I have an award I would like to give to Rear Admiral Ikanovich. Admiral if you wouldn't mind stepping up on the dais here I have something for you that I am sure you will cherish with all of your heart," asked the president.

Zakkova made his way to the dais and was soon standing next to the president not knowing what to expect.

"Rear Admiral Ikanovich it is with extreme pleasure and pride that I hereby award you the highest award possible this country can bestow on a citizen or warrior such as you. Admiral I hereby award you the Medal of Honor for eliminating from this planet two of America's most dangerous enemies," said the president as he put the Medal of Honor around Zakkova's huge neck. The crowd erupted in applause and started chanting Zakkova's name.

"Ladies and gentlemen I accept this vaunted award with honor and gratuity for the chance to serve my country. Being a U.S. Navy SEAL is one of the highest honors a man can achieve. It has been my pleasure and my pride to serve with the SEALs the last fifteen years of my life. I love the SEALs and I love all of my brothers in the SEALs. I will miss the men I served with and the dangerous missions we were given. It is my firm belief that God has guided my path of righteousness on all of my missions. So God I thank you and I thank you Mr. President for bestowing this honor on me today."

"You're very welcomed Zakkova. Now I believe you have some awards that you would like to bestow."

"Yes I do Mr. President, thank you. Men, when you hear your name please come up to the dais. Lieutenant Michael Sanders. Lieutenant it is my honor to award you the Silver Star for valor and your performance on our last mission."

Zakkova hung the Silver Star around the lieutenant's neck and then called the other ten SEALs up to the dais one by one to be awarded their Silver Stars. When he was done he thanked the president and the SEALs were greeted with a loud round of applause.

After the awards ceremony every one drank Champaign and ate hors d'oeuvres as they mingled with the crowd. The president's Chief of Staff walked up to Zakkova and shook his hand.

"Zakkova, congratulations on your recent mission and your promotion and last but not least your Medal of Honor award. The president and some other people would like to meet with you in the Oval

Office in about thirty minutes. You're all cleared through security so just walk on in. Do you remember how to get there from here?"

"I'd be honored to meet with the president in his office. I've been in that office so many times over the years that I know it like the back of my hand."

"Good, we'll see you there then."

Thirty minutes later Zakkova found himself in the Oval Office. In attendance were Mitch Daniels, the president, Paul West the vice president, the president's Chief of Staff, Doug Michaels, David Peters, the Director of the CIA, Leon Smith the Pentagon chief, Keith Davids, the Director of the NSA, General Martin Sherman, the Chairman of the Joint Chiefs of Staff, Admiral Harward, Janet Meredith, the Secretary of Homeland Security and Jane Cochran, the Secretary of State. Zakkova wondered what was going on. Why did these important people want to meet with him?

"Thank you for taking out the time to meet with us, Admiral. I must say that that video of you killing al-Zawahiri was mesmerizing. I must have watched that thing twenty times. That cobra is amazing. It was impressive when he spit venom in al-Zawahiri's eyes. That video is the most watched video on YouTube. Maybe it will help recruit some future SEALs. It was good PR to release it Admiral Harward. Look, Zakkova, we have a proposal for you that I think you might find to your liking. You know as well as anyone the threats we face in this world. We have the Islamic fascist terrorists who want to kill us all, the Iranians who are developing nuclear weapons and have vowed to wipe Israel off the map, Mexican drug cartels that are invading our southern borders and bringing violence and narcotics with them, Bashar al-Assad who's slaughtering his own people and providing weapons to Hezbollah and Hamas who are using those weapons to attack Israel, and numerous insane heads of state that are creating an unstable world. We in this room are bound by our duties to make this nation safe from all of those ills. Over your career you have removed many threats that were hostile to the United States. For that we are internally grateful. But as you also know these remaining threats are getting larger and more aggressive in their stance. We could overtly or covertly deal with these threats but for geopolitical reasons we can't take action against them. That's where you come in. We would like to hire you and men of your choosing to eliminate these threats. If you do it as a private citizen, we could claim plausible deniability and keep our hands clean. How does this sound to you so far Zakkova?" asked the president.

"I know firsthand that the threats you are speaking of are real. We have many foreign enemies who would like nothing better than to give us another 9/11 or worse. I like your proposal. It would keep me in the game. After all I am only thirty-five-years-old. There are things that you need to consider first, though. Missions against these threats will be very expensive running into the millions of dollars. Also, I would need immunity from prosecution on the federal, state, local and international levels for crimes I may commit. That means I would be untouchable to law enforcement agencies, Interpol and your Attorney General."

"Zakkova, cost is no issue. We would be prepared to pay you and men that you hire millions of dollars to remove these threats. Your immunity to prosecution is no issue either. I will issue a mandate making that possible. Do we have to pay for your snake, too?"

"Ah, ah, ah, no you just have to supply him with plenty of milk chocolate. That damn snake loves chocolate. Weirdest thing I've ever seen."

"There are heads of state that we would want eliminated. Would that pose a problem for you Zakkova?" asked David Peters.

"Not at all, I have a few heads of state on my list that I would like to eliminate."

"Zakkova, do you have nonmilitary men you could use to help on some of these missions?" asked Leon Smith.

"Oh yes, I have an active network of former SEALS, Special Forces personnel, SAS, MI6 and Mossad agents I can activate with a phone call."

"It's settled then. We'll have the immunity documents drafted and signed by me and the Attorney General. David here will be your go to guy. He will contact you when we have a mission for you to perform. Do you have any further questions, Zakkova?" asked the President Romney.

"Yes, I will need full and unfettered access to CIA and NSA intel and NSA satellite and communications surveillance data when I need it. Also, we need to put a persona to this thing. If I carry out these missions and no one takes responsibility for them, the world leaders will automatically accuse the U.S. or Israel of these deeds. We need to come up with a name for a type of world vigilante organization that we will publicize and take responsibility for these crimes against states. As time goes by it will gain notoriety and a mystic fame. Eyes will look elsewhere other than the U.S. or Israel as the perpetrator. David, why don't you have your analysts come up with a name for our little group?"

"That's an excellent idea, Zakkova. I didn't think of that but you are right. Everyone will blame us for any hostile actions against foreign states or rogue criminal enterprises. And of course you will have full access to all CIA, NSA, Homeland Security information and assets and any Air Force assets you may need," said the president.

"I second that offer for the CIA," said David Peters.

"We're all in at the NSA," said Keith Alexander.

"Count Homeland Security in," said Janet Meredith.

"Well then, I think our intelligence assets and Zakkova's skills will make a good match. I look forward to your first mission, Zakkova," said the president.

"It will be my pleasure to continue serving my country on an ongoing basis and to plan and execute missions to remove our threats," said Zakkova as he got up and shook hands with everyone in the office.

Chapter 4

Zakkova was a millionaire many times over. He had been very successful trading index options and currencies while he was in the SEALs. This same intelligence of the markets also carried over academically. Zakkova had managed to earn PHDs in nuclear physics and computer science from MIT while in the SEALs.

Zakkova's wealth enabled him to own a highly modified Gulfstream G650 and Jet Ranger helicopter. The G650 had high performance Rolls Royce engines, advanced avionics, a Distributed Aperture System (DAS) missile approach warning system, six AIM-6 Sidewinder missiles mounted on a deployable rotary launch system in the cargo compartment, two Hellfire missiles hidden in the wing fuel pods, and chaff and flare dispesnsers. He had been building a 20,000 square foot mansion on five acres of land in Carmel California. He also owned his own private island off the coast of Florida that would be outfitted with the same mansion and security systems he was putting into place at Carmel. Zakkova was installing his own designed security system for his properties in Carmel and his island. He had already installed surveillance cameras and motion detectors all throughout his properties and in his mansion. He also installed hundreds of land mines throughout his properties. The mansions had glass turrets on the roofs that gave a 360 degree view of all of his properties. These served as the main security stations. The land mines, thanks to Inverse Technologies, were remotely controlled. The security station had a large thirty-six inch display that showed the location of each land mine. They showed up as orange dots on the display and on the buttons that triggered each mine. They had sensors on them that revealed when something was in the blast radius of a mine. When this happened, the orange dots turned green on the display and on the buttons. When there was a green button, Zakkova could detonate the mine by pushing the button. The system also had an automatic feature. Zakkova could set the system on automatic and the land mines would automatically detonate when something was within the blast radius. This was a good feature because if a large force invaded the property to attack the mansion, Zakkova could just set the system on automatic and let the mines detonate without having to push buttons to detonate them. The glass turret also enabled Zakkova to use his sniper rifle and missile launcher on any hostiles that invaded his properties.

Zakkova loved speed. He had a 2004 Mustang Cobra with a 2.8 Kenne Bell supercharger on it and other high performance equipment. The Cobra put out 750 horse power and 725 foot pounds of torque. Zakkova also had a custom made motorcycle with an R&R 155cc twin cam engine on it. The bike could run the quarter mile in 8.5 seconds with Zakkova on it and 7.2 seconds with a 170 pound man on it. Zakkova loved to drive his Cobra and ride his motorcycle.

It was a warm sunny day and Zakkova decided to ride his motorcycle into Carmel to see what was going on. By this time Zakkova had let his jet black hair grow down to his shoulders. He didn't like to wear a helmet even though it was required by law in California. He liked to let his long black hair just blow in the wind when he rode his bike.

Zakkova came upon a garage with a line of choppers parked outside. He decided to drop in and introduce himself. The sound of Zakkova's powerful motorcycle brought a number of men outside to see who it was.

"Good morning gentlemen. My name is Zakkova Ikanovich. I just moved here and decided to drop in to say hello. Anybody who loves bikes as much as I do is a friend to me," said Zakkova.

The men just stood there in awe of Zakkova's magnificent body and awesome motorcycle.

"Hi, Zakkova, my name is Clyde Munroe and I'm the owner of this garage and president of our motorcycle club. We call ourselves the Nomads. That is a one hell of a bike you got there."

"Thanks Clyde. She's my love and joy. How many members do you have in your club?"

"There are fifteen of us and we all work at the garage when we're not out doing club business."

"I suppose your club business is running guns. Do you have competition with that from rival gangs?"

"No, we pretty much have a monopoly on guns. The rival gangs such as the Aztecs and the Red Devils are mostly in the drug and prostitution trade. We keep drug trafficking and prostitution out of Carmel. For that, the sheriff cuts us a little slack. It's the ATF we have to worry about the most."

"Who's your supplier?"

"We have a good agreement with the IRA. They supply us with top-of-the-line high quality weapons that we mostly sell to other motorcycle gangs and drug traffickers as well as the occasional hit man. "

"Ah, the IRA. I know they have access to good weapons and are eager to sell them to the highest bidder to finance their operation."

"Yeah, we pay top dollar for the guns we buy from the IRA and then mark them up 50%. They're expensive but the gangs here and in Nevada will gladly pay high prices to get their hands on AK47s, HK 53s and MP3s. It's been a lucrative business for us. We justify it by assuring the gangs will use the weapons to kill other gang members. So you might call it a stretch and say we perform a community service."

"Well, that's good to hear. And it's noble of you to keep the drug trade and prostitution out of this beautiful town. If you ever have a security problem or problems with a rival gang, let me know and maybe I can help you out on that. I'm an ex-U.S. Navy SEAL and I know how to take out threats."

"Wow, an ex-SEAL. That is awesome Zakkova. Thanks for your offer, too. We may have to take you up on that in the future. This is a dangerous business we're in and there is always another gang who tries to move in on us."

"Consider yourself protected now. My place is just north of here right off the Pacific Coast Highway. Come visit me sometime. You and all of your guys will always be welcomed there. We can pull back a few beers and trade war stories."

"Thanks, Zakkova. I can't wait to see your place. I've heard about it. It sounds as awesome as you are."

"Okay, then, I think I'll make my way into town see what's going on. Have a good day Clyde."

"Same to you Zakkova. Hope to see you again soon."

Zakkova made his way into Carmel. At a stop sign he pulled up beside a beautiful brunet in a Mercedes SL 600 convertible.

"Hey, babe, nice ride you got there," said Zakkova to the woman.

"Well, hi stranger. I haven't seen you in our cozy little town before."

"I'm new here. My name is Zakkova."

"And my name is Lola. I hope I see you again soon. Your bike is as awesome as your body."

"You're not bad yourself," said Zakkova as the light turned green and he sped off toward town.

Zakkova pulled into the Sheriff's office so he could introduce himself to local law enforcement. He got off of his bike and strode into the Sheriff's office like he owned the place. He walked up to the counter and asked the deputy if the Sheriff was in.

"Yes, he's in. Whom may I say is calling?" asked the deputy.

"My name is Zakkova Ikanovich. I'm new in town and just wanted to introduce myself to the Sheriff."

"Hold on a minute and I'll tell him you're here," said the deputy as he stood up and walked down the center hallway.

"He's available. Just follow me."

Zakkova followed the deputy to the Sheriff's office and walked in.

"Hello, Sheriff, my name is Zakkova Ikanovich. I'm new in town and just wanted to introduce myself to you."

"Nice to meet you, Zakkova, I'm Sheriff Noles" said the Sheriff as he stood up and shook Zakkova's hand.

"This must be the most beautiful town in the country. I built myself a big spread just outside of town off Pacific Coast Highway. I hope you're keeping a low crime rate here."

"Oh, yeah, not much big happens here. We have our usual domestic disputes and the local drunks to contend with but it's pretty much petty crimes we deal with."

"That's good to here. I met your local biker club and they seem like a pretty good bunch of guys."

"Yeah, you must be talking about the Nomads. They run guns and they're good at it. I haven't been able to get a bust on them for that and the ATF is trying like hell to. But we really have a détente with them. They keep drug trafficking and prostitution out of Carmel and we turn our eye on their gun running. It's worked out pretty well. A number of drug runners have tried to set up shop here and run meth labs but the Nomads always shut them down and chase them out of town. They can do things we can't do without a bunch of warrants."

"Sounds like a win-win situation to me. I offered them my services if they ever have a problem with a rival gang. I'm an ex-U.S. Navy SEAL so I know how to keep bad things from happening. I'm offering my help to you, too, if you need it as long as it is not against the Nomads. Here's a number at Langley you can call to find out all about me. They will tell you that I am untouchable, not that I'm planning any crimes or anything. My one vice is riding my motorcycle without a helmet. So after you call Langley, tell your deputies to not stop me for riding without a helmet. It's been nice meeting with you Sheriff. I look forward to helping you with any big problems that may crop up," said Zakkova as he stood up to shake the Sheriff's hand.

"It's been nice meeting you, too, Zakkova. I'll be sure to call Langley as you suggested. I'll tell my deputies to let you slide on the helmet thing."

Chapter 5

When Zakkova got home he saw that the light on the red phone was flashing. This was a hotline to the president's and CIA Director's offices.

"Zakkova here."

"Zakkova, this is Dave. We need your help. We have a mission for you that is of utmost importance. How soon can you get to the Oval Office?"

"Hi, Dave, all I need to do is file a flight plan for the Gulfstream. I can be there in about three hours."

"Excellent, please hurry. We'll all be waiting for you."

"No problem. As soon as I hang up I'll head to the airport."

Zakkova arrived at the White House around 5:00 PM that day. Awaiting him in the Oval Office where the president, the Directors of the CIA and NSA and the Joint Chiefs of Staff.

"Zakkova, thank you very much for coming on such short notice. We have a mission we would like to discuss with you," said the president.

"It's no problem. Fortunately I caught a tail wind and made good progress here. I'm anxious to hear what you have in mind."

"Well, as you know Iran has been working on developing a nuclear weapon. They have over 10,000 centrifuges set up and are refining uranium to weapons grade 90%. Their main facility for doing this is located at Qom. Israel is just itching to strike Iran at any moment. Unfortunately, the Iranians have burrowed their centrifuges so far under the ground that our bunker busters cannot even penetrate them. That's where you come in. We need you to get inside their Qom facility and sabotage the centrifuges at Qom before Israel pulls the trigger and causes a full out war across the Middle East."

"Yes, I am aware of what Iran has been doing to conceal and protect their centrifuges. My estimate is that they'll have enough enriched uranium to make four nukes within ten months. They'll get the plutonium they need from the spent reactor rods from their nuclear reactor at Bushehr. I gladly accept this mission but I need to make a few phone calls to find out if the men I will need for this are available."

"Of course, I understand. Could you call them now? You can call them from my office with me on speaker to lend some credibility and urgency to this," said the president.

"Credibility is of no concern. They all trust me implicitly. However, they like to keep their anonymity. So if you'll just get me a sat phone I'll make the calls now in one of your empty offices."

"I understand the anonymity issue. Hang on and I'll get you the sat phone immediately."

The president gave Zakkova a sat phone and he went into an empty office and made his calls to a couple of ex-SEAL an SAS officers and his retired Mossad contact. Within twenty minutes the calls were made and each man was glad to accept the mission. Zakkova went back to the Oval Office to brief the president on his calls.

"I've made contact with some of my men and they all readily accepted the mission. Here's the deal though. It will cost you $50,000,000 to take out the centrifuges. If you want to take out the Grand Ayatollah Sayyed Ali Hosseini Khamenei and President Mahmoud Ahmadinejad too, it will cost you $100,000,000. To do that, we'll have to stay in country for at least two weeks. That increases the risk of us getting captured immensely. But I highly recommend you take this option. The younger Iranians are starting to revolt and they hate Ahmadinejad. If we can help them by taking out their president, then I think there will be a good chance of a regime change with our help. This will be a chance for Iran to become a democracy instead of a theocracy."

"That is a good point, Zakkova. But do you really think you can take out Grand Ayatollah Sayyed Ali Hosseini Khamenei and Ahmadinejad? The security surrounding them is awfully tight."

"If we didn't think we could do it, we wouldn't have presented this option. But that's why it will take some time to do. Two weeks in country for the whole operation should be adequate."

"I agree with your proposal Zakkova. If you can take out the centrifuges at Qom and Grand Ayatollah Sayyed Ali Hosseini Khamenei and Ahmadinejad, that will pretty much neuter Iran's nuclear program. $100,000,000 is a fair price for this that we'll gladly pay. To where shall we send the money?"

"Send half of it to this numbered account in the Cayman Islands. We'll collect the second half after we complete the job. It will take about three weeks to plan the mission and get the assets we need in position."

"That sounds fair to me. It's a deal then," says the president.

"David, have your men come up with a good name for our operators?" asked Zakkova

"Yes we have, Zakkova. We would like to call the group "Mission for World Peace."

"That's a good name. I'll contact you when we're ready to infiltrate Iran. I will need to look at the most recent sat photos of Qom."

"No problem, Zakkova. How about you come with to my office tomorrow morning at 8:30 AM and we'll spend the day looking over the photos we have," said Keith Alexander the Director of the NSA.

"Sounds like a plan. And Martin, I'll need a MC130H on this mission."

"Just tell me when and where, Zakkova, and it will be available."

"Iran has high security at all of their centrifuge sites. How will you get in, Zakkova?" asked the Director of the CIA.

"Better you didn't know. Plausible deniability means you don't have access to our plans and methods."

"Will there be a lot of collateral damage?" asked Jane Cochran, the Secretary of State.

"There are probably over two hundred scientists and workers at Qom. They will all be killed."

"Well, I guess you could say they are all working on a weapon of mass destruction to use against the U.S. and Israel so the casualties are justified," said the president.

"That's a good way to put it, Mr. President. After we accomplish the mission I will send David video of the attack. Get this video to the public right away. Using YouTube would probably be best. It should be narrated by someone with an Arabic accent to keep the public guessing as to who the Mission for World Peace people really are."

"That is an excellent idea, Zakkova. Get us the video and we'll get it out there right away," said David.

"Okay, good luck and God speed on our first mission, Zakkova," said the president as he stood up to shake Zakkova's hand.

Chapter 6

Zakkova flew his Gulfstream G650 back to Carmel that the next afternoon after meeting with Keith Alexander to go over the sat photos of Qom. When he got home he immediately got out his sat phone and called the four men he wanted for this mission. He connected with all four men and scheduled a meeting at his house two days from then.

The men arrived on schedule and made their way to Zakkova's mansion. Zakkova had selected Sammy Watters, an ex-U.S. Navy SEAL, Mark Bunting, another ex-SEAL, Don Jacobs, an ex-SAS operator and Shalom Rabin, an ex-Mossad agent. They arrived with much excitement that they would be working with Zakkova on an important mission.

When the two cars they were using arrived at Zakkova's mansion, Zakkova's security system let him know they had arrived.

"Good morning gentlemen. Thank you all for coming and volunteering for this mission. As you know, Iran is getting closer and closer to developing a nuclear weapon that they will surely use against Israel. If they get one developed, the dynamics in the Middle East will change dramatically and the threat to U.S. and Israeli interests will increase immensely. With a nuclear weapon in their arsenal Iran will be able to target Israel for extinction and blackmail its Arab neighbors. In addition, Saudi Arabia and other Arab nations will want to develop their own nuclear weapons, a situation the U.S. cannot tolerate. The young Iranians are starting to revolt against the strict Sharia laws of the mullahs. And the sanctions the U.S. and European nations have put on Iran are making the Iranian people very upset with their rulers. So in addition to taking out the centrifuges at Qom, we will also assassinate

Grand Ayatollah Sayyed Ali Hosseini Khamenei and Ahmadinejad," said Zakkova.

"But how will we get into the nuclear facility at Qom?" asked Sammy.

"Good question. We'll cross into Iran from the Iraqi border. Sat photos have shown us the type of uniforms and vehicles the Quds use. The Quds wield tremendous military power and provide security for all of Iran's classified facilities. We'll go in as QUDs officers with one of us posing as scientist and infiltrate the centrifuges. We'll have false Quds credentials and a special order from Ahmadinejad to deliver some test equipment that should allow us access to the centrifuges. One of us will be dressed in a white lab coat and play the part of the scientist. We'll tell the guards at Qom that Dr. Ibn has a special delivery for the facility."

"But Zakkova, Qom is heavily fortified. There will be keypads, fingerprint and retina scanners at all of the facilities' doors. How will we get past those?" asked Don.

"Oh, that's where my special friend Jake at Inverse Technologies comes in. He has made a device that will attach to the keypads and electronically determine what the passcodes are. He also has devices that will fool the fingerprint and retina scanners into opening the locks."

"How will we take out the centrifuges?" asked Mark.

"The scientist will be delivering a white cabinet on caster wheels to the centrifuges. The cabinet will be loaded with one thousand pounds of Semtex plastic explosives with a remote controlled detonator. The scientist will take the cabinet down to the centrifuges and just leave it in the hallway outside of the room where the centrifuges are. It will look like a piece of lab equipment so it should draw no attention. Once we're out of the underground facility, we will detonate the Semtex. One thousand pounds of Semtex should collapse the entire underground facility. Here are some sat photos of the complex. The centrifuges are located in this mountain here. They are thirty floors under the base of the mountain and that's why our bunker busters can't destroy them. This fence is about ten feet tall with razor wire at the top. There are two guards at the gate. The gate is about twenty yards from the entrance to the mountain."

"Only two guards? That doesn't sound like much to protect a secured facility like this," said Sammy.

"Because the inside of the facility is so well secured they don't think anyone could enter it even if they got past the guards at the gate," said Zakkova.

"That sounds like a good plan. Now how will we get to Grand Ayatollah Sayyed Khamenei and Ahmadinejad?" asked Shalom.

"We'll do what we do best. We recon the Grand Ayatollah Sayyed Ali Hosseini Khamenei's and Ahmadinejad's movements and then decide the best way to take them out. We'll take them out by sniper fire, set explosives to their limos and blow him up, or do a clandestine attack on their houses and kill them at point blank range. I am having the Quds uniforms and vehicles prepared now. I expect we'll have everything ready to go in about a week. We'll travel to Bagdad and from there we'll fly in an MC-130 gun ship to the Iranian border. Our vehicle will be four wheel drive so we'll cross border off the main highways and drive through the desert until we get to Kermanshah which will take us to Qom. We'll spend a day reconning Qom to make sure we don't miss something that could ruin our plan. As soon as we blow up the centrifuges, we'll head to Tehran and start reconning Grand Ayatollah Sayyed Ali Hosseini Khamenei and Ahmadinejad. It may take a few days to kill Grand Ayatollah Sayyed Ali Hosseini Khamenei and Ahmadinejad because after we blow up the centrifuges security will be heighten around them. We'll take our time and wait for the best shot. We may have to stay in Tehran for two weeks to get the job done. We're being paid $100,000,000 to perform this mission so it's a big pay day. I've received a $50,000,000 down payment. Before you leave, give me your bank account numbers and I'll wire $10,000,000 into your accounts. Do all of you accept this mission?"

"Aye, I accept," said Don.

"I'm in," said Sammy.

"Big payday, I wouldn't miss if for the world," said Shalom.

"Count me in. I hate those Iranian bastards," said Mark.

"Very good, I have no doubt that we'll be successful. Now would you guys like a tour of my house. I'm sure you'll be impressed with my security system."

Zakkova took them on a tour of his mansion. They were amazed at his security system, especially the remote land mines. They also liked his firing range. He had built a building two hundred yards long. Inside the building there were separate firing ranges for knife throwing, bow and arrow shooting, pistol shooting and sniper rifle shooting. When the tour was done, Zakkova sent the men home.

"Okay men, we'll all meet in Bagdad in seven days. Check into the Bagdad Marriott downtown. You don't have to bring anything with you. All of our gear for the mission will be flown into Bagdad on a C-17," said Zakkova.

Chapter 7

Seven days later Zakkova flew to Bagdad in his Gulfstream. FAA regulations required a co-pilot for a G650. Zakkova didn't need a co-pilot to fly the plane but he decided to bring one along to guard and take care of the aircraft in Bagdad while Zakkova and the other men were on their mission. Zakkova chose Jimmy Valentine an ex-USAF fighter pilot that he had worked many missions on together. Jimmy had a license to fly twin engine jet aircraft and had already been checked out on the Gulfstream G650. Besides it would be a long trip and Zakkova would welcome some company to go over the mission with. Jimmy was more than happy to accompany Zakkova on this mission and readily accepted Zakkova's payment terms.

Zakkova made good time to Bagdad. He flew nonstop because the G650 had a range of 6,500 miles. When he arrived in Bagdad he was happy to find his team was already there and waiting for him.

"What's next Zakkova?" asked Sammy.

"I need to meet with Colonel David Smith to check on our equipment for the mission and to make sure the MC-130H is here and ready to transport us to the border."

Zakkova found the military headquarters at Bagdad's airport and entered the complex. He went to the front counter that was manned by a U.S. Army lieutenant.

"Greetings lieutenant, I am Zakkova Ikanovich and I'm here to see Colonel David Smith."

"Oh yes, Mr. Ikanovich the Colonel has been expecting you. Let's go make sure he's not tied up on the phone," said the lieutenant as they made their way to Colonel Smith's office.

"Hello Zakkova. I'm Colonel Smith. It is a pleasure to meet you. I've heard so many good things about you," said the Colonel as he shook Zakkova's hand.

"And it's my deepest pleasure to meet you Colonel Smith. We've been counting on you to provide the equipment we need for the mission."

"I'm pleased to tell you all of your requested equipment is ready and the MC-130H is on the tarmac ready to take you to the border. Follow me and I'll show you what we've been able to do."

Colonel Smith led Zakkova out to a waiting Humvee and first made their way to where Zakkova's men were waiting to be picked up. After introductions were made, the Colonel drove to a hanger on the far left side of the airport. The men climbed out of the Humvee and made their way into the hanger.

Colonel Smith showed them the equipment they would be using.

"The vehicle is an exact replica of the ones the Quds use. Same make and model with official markings on it. Over here are the Quds uniforms. It was hard to replicate these because the sat photos were somewhat blurred but we think we have a pretty good likeness that should raise no alarms."

Zakkova walked over and inspected the vehicle and the uniforms. He pulled out the sat photos and compared them to the Colonel's work.

"Good job Colonel. The vehicle is a perfect match and the uniforms look real good. We should have no problem fooling the guards at Qom. Do you also have our special delivery package ready to go?"

"Yes I do. Walk this way and I'll show you."

The Colonel led the men to a back room and unlocked the door. In the middle of the room sat a white cabinet that was ten feet long and five feet wide.

"That's your gift to the Iranians. It contains one thousand pounds of Semtex surrounded by hundreds of metal balls. There should be enough explosive power in here to take down the whole mountain. As you requested, it also has a remote detonator so you can ignite the Semtex at the proper time. Here's the cell phone that goes with the remote detonator. Just push the three key twice and you'll have a nice fireworks display."

"This is excellent Colonel. My thanks to you and your men for preparing all of this. Because of your hard work this mission will be successful. When can we take the MC-130H to the border?"

"It's ready when you are. Just say the word and the pilots will have it ready to go."

"Since it's late in the afternoon, we should spend the night here and get some good rest and then be ready to depart at 0800 hours tomorrow morning."

"I think that is a good idea, Zakkova. I'll set you up in the barracks on the base here and make sure you get plenty of chow."

"Thank you for your hospitality Colonel. It is much appreciated. I will pass on a commendation for you and your men back in D.C."

"Well thank you Zakkova. It is always my pleasure to serve men of your caliber. If you need anything else, just let me know and I will get it for you. Good luck on your mission and God speed. You will be doing the world a great favor."

The men checked into the barracks and put their kits in secured lockers. After eating a big dinner in the mess hall, the men met in an empty office in the barracks to go over the mission plan one more time. When everyone was assured what role they would play and how it would all go down at Qom they went over the plans to take out Khamenei and Ahmadinejad. This would be the hardest part of the mission. They would have to act fast right after they blew up the centrifuges. Security would no doubt be tightened after the explosion. Once word leaked out that Grand Ayatollah Sayyed Ali Hosseini Khamenei was assassinated the mullahs would go to underground safe houses and stay there until the perpetrators were caught. This would essentially leave Iran without a government. It was a risky proposition but Zakkova was sure they could do it with proper planning.

After reviewing the mission plans, the men went to bed early to get as much sleep as possible before the big day ahead. The excitement brewing in each man made it difficult to sleep but they all got at least six hours of sound sleep.

Chapter 8

At 0800 hours the men boarded the MC-130H and headed for the border. It took about ninety minutes for the MC-130H to fly to the coordinates Zakkova gave the pilots. The area at the border was hard packed sand so the MC-130H had no problem landing.

Once the MC-130H landed and came to a stop the men sprang into action. The loadmaster released the handle to the rear cargo door and lowered the ramp so the men could drive the vehicle off of the plane. The MC-130H landed on the border about forty kilometers from Kermanshah. They would drive through the desert to Kermanshah to avoid any check points. At Kermanshah they would get on the main roads that would take them to Qom. It would be about an eight hour drive to Qom. That meant that they would arrive at Qom at about 01500 hours, which was a good time because most of the scientists and workers would be taking a dinner break. That would mean less eyes to scrutinize what they were going to do.

The men arrived at Qom on schedule and pulled up to the main gate of the complex. There were two guards at the gate. The men stopped their vehicle at the gate and waited for the guards to come and see what they wanted.

In perfect Farsi with no accent Zakkova told the main guard, "Good morning comrade. We have Dr. Ibn with us who has some very important equipment to deliver and set up for the centrifuges."

The guard was immediately taken aback by their Quds uniforms and the immense size of Zakkova and the fact that he was posing as a four star general.

"Good morning. Do you have the proper documentation to gain entrance to the facility," asked the guard.

"Yes we do. It is signed by President Ahmadinejad himself," said Zakkova as he passed the forged documents to the guard.

The guard read the documents carefully and then looked inside the vehicle to make sure nothing was amiss. He looked at Dr. Ibn dressed in a white lab coat and was satisfied that he was indeed an Iranian scientist. He then inspected the cargo very carefully to make sure there we no hidden explosives attached to it.

"What is in the cabinet?" asked the guard.

"We can't give you much detail because it is highly classified. We can tell you, though, that the device will speed up the enrichment process by almost 100%. That means we should have enough enriched uranium to build our first nuclear weapon way ahead of schedule, which praise Allah we will use it to destroy Israel."

"Amen to that brother. Okay, you are cleared to enter the facility. We will remotely open the steel doors in the mountain from here so you can drive into the complex. You will need to know the cipher lock combination and your thumbprints and retinas must match the thumbprint and retina scans in the data base before you can enter the elevator to take you down the centrifuges. Once you are thirty floors underground you will take a long hallway to get the centrifuges. I take it that you know the cipher lock combination and that your thumbprint and retina scans are in the database. Only one person at a time can go through the doors. There are scanners in the door frame that will detect multiple persons trying to pass through the doorway at once. If that happens, an alarm will go off and the door will shut and all of the security measures will lock up so no one else can enter the facility."

'Yes, we understand the protocols and we have all been cleared to enter the facility," said Zakkova.

"Well, then, you are cleared to enter. Good luck with setting up your device. I hope it works."

"It will work for sure. We have done extensive testing with it. It won't take long to set up. We should be back within twenty minutes."

The men's vehicle entered the complex and headed for the steel doors in the mountain. When they got within twenty feet of the doors they opened to a loading dock and the elevator that would take them down to the centrifuges. There were no guards on duty inside the loading dock, which made their entry that much easier.

They backed the vehicle up to the loading dock to make unloading the heavy cabinet much easier.

Once the men unloaded the cabinet, they went to the service elevator and withdrew three devices that Jake at Inverse Technologies gave Zakkova. The first device was a designed for the keypad cipher. It would quickly process thousands of numbers until it came up with the cipher combination. Zakkova put the device over the keypad and it almost immediately found the correct sequence of numbers and keyed them in. The cipher lock was now unlocked. Next, Zakkova placed a device over the thumbprint scanner. This device would hack into the database and provide a thumbprint image of the last person who placed their thumb on the scanner. A green light flashed on indicating that the thumbprint was valid. The last device worked similar to the thumbprint device. It also hacked into the database and retrieved the last retina scan and scanned it into the scanner. Another green light flashed on indicating a valid retina scan. With all security measures met, a green light came on top of the elevator and the door opened. Sammy was the first person through. Zakkova repeated the process for each of the remaining men of the team and for himself. They were all in the elevator now and pushed the thirty button to take the elevator down to the centrifuges.

When they got to the thirtieth floor, the door opened and there was a long hallway like the guard said. They moved quickly down the hallway and opened the door to the room where the centrifuges were. There were 10,000 centrifuges churning away. None of the people paid much attention to Zakkova and his men. They were too involved with what they were doing to care. Shalom wheeled the cabinet into the middle of the room and placed it next to another large piece of test equipment. The men went back down the hallway to the elevator and took it back to the loading dock on the first floor. They stopped on every fifth floor to put a signal booster on the wall outside of the elevator to make sure the cell phone signal would penetrate thirty floors underground to the detonator on the Semtex. These where small two inch by two inch gray plastic devices that had adhesive backs on them. They also put a larger one on the outside of the main door to the building to penetrate the steel core door. Jake at Inverse Technologies had provided these to Zakkova and his men. When they got to the ground floor they got into their vehicle and drove back to the main gate.

"Okay men, we need to take these guards out so they can't identify us later. Sammy, Mark be ready when we stop to put a bullet in the heads of each guard," says Zakkova.

When they got to the gate, the two guards came out of the of the guard house to meet them. The guards approached the vehicle on each side. Sammy shot the guard on the driver's side with his silenced Desert Eagle pistol. This gun shot 50 caliber hollow point bullets so one shot to the head literally blew the head off the guard. At the same time, Mark shot the guard on the passenger's side of the vehicle with his silenced SIG P226 pistol. Both guards were now dead.

"Damn Sammy, that gun is a fucking canon. It can do some real damage," said Zakkova.

"Yeah man, the bigger the better is what I always say. I love this baby."

"Okay Shalom, let's set off the Semtex and blow this place to pieces. And Mark, make sure you get a good video of this."

"Shalom pushed the three key on the cell phone twice. The explosion was loud and devastating. The shock wave lifted the vehicle off of the ground about ten inches. The steel doors were blown off the side of the mountain and then the whole mountain collapsed. There were flames and a lot of smoke, dust and debris flying everywhere. The Qom centrifuge facility was reduced to a pile of rubble. Because the centrifuges were thirty floors underground, there was little risk of radiation poison leaking into the atmosphere.

"Mission accomplished men. We just did something even the Israelis couldn't do. Everything went as planned, just perfect. Now comes the hard part. We've got to take out those crazy bastards the Grand Ayatollah Sayyed Ali Hosseini Khamenei and President Ahmadinejad. Let's head for Tehran and start our recon of the Grand Ayatollah Sayyed Ali Hosseini Khamenei. Mark, send he video of this little adventure to David at the CIA now. I want the world to know that Iran just suffered a severe setback to their nuclear weapons program," said Zakkova.

When David received the video he was stunned and very happy. He had no idea that Zakkova and his men could wreak that much havoc on Iran's Qom centrifuge facility. He immediately called the president to tell him the good news.

"Mr. President, good news. Zakkova and his men just completely destroyed Qom's centrifuge facility. I just received the video from them. It's awesome. I'm sending it to you right now."

"I got it David. My God, what devastation, our guys took down the whole mountain. This is a real win for us. The Israelis will be happy and probably be a little jealous. This won't be another Chernobyl will it?"

"No, Mr. President, the centrifuges were thirty floors underground so the radiation fallout will be trapped underground."

"That's terrific, David. When are you going to release the video to the public?"

"The script for the narration has already been written, I'll get our Arab agent to record the audio track for it now and then dub it into the video. The video will be released within the hour."

"Okay, that's wonderful David. The Iranians probably won't believe it but who cares? The world will have some new heroes to celebrate."

As planned, David released the video within the hour. The narrative was very convincing.

Hello peaceful people of the world. Our name is Mission for World Peace. We exist because no government can take out deadly threats to peace. We are a completely independent organization whose charter is to eliminate hostile activities being undertaken by any government or terrorist organization. We will give peaceful people a reason to cheer for the elimination of all evil elements in the world. Today we destroyed Iran's nuclear centrifuges at their facility in Qom. Iran was enriching uranium to 90% weapons grade material there. As you know, Iran is hell bent on developing a nuclear war head to destroy Israel and threaten the interest of the United States. This act of ours will set Iran's nuclear ambitions back by years. The destruction of the centrifuges at Qom killed Iran's nuclear scientists, a devastating blow to their program. We are warning all countries, terrorist cells and crime cartels that your days are numbered. We will act decisively to stop your nefarious ways. Mission for World Peace is afraid of no one and will take on and destroy any threat to world peace. Peaceful people of the world you now have a guardian angel on your side. May God bless you and bring you everlasting peace.

The video quickly became the most watched video on YouTube and other news outlets. People around the world cheered this latest development and couldn't wait to hear more from the Mission for World Peace. Of course, Iran wasn't buying any of it. They immediately cast blame on the U.S. and Israel and filed a complaint with the UN Security Council. They also threaten to block the Strait of Hormuz so no oil tankers could pass through with their cargo. They claimed that over three hundred civilians were killed in the blast. They vowed retribution against the U.S. and Israel. But both the U.S. and Israel issued statements that they were not the perpetrators of this attack and warned Iran that any attack on US and Israeli interests would be dealt with harshly.

Chapter 9

The next day the men reconned the Grand Ayatollah Sayyed Ali Hosseini Khamenei house and office to determine the best means of attacking him and killing Khamenei.

Khamenei's house was a two story stucco mansion surrounded by a twelve foot stucco wall topped with razor wire. The mansion was set back about two hundred yards from the main gate in the wall.

"Okay men, I think we'll just walk through the front door on this one. We'll tell the guards there has been a credible threat against Khamenei's life and we're here to make sure the mansion is secure. We'll show them a directive for the inspection from President Ahmadinejad. That coming from a four star general in the Quds, the guards at the gate will do whatever I ask them to do. We've got to clean house, though. There can be no survivors after we're done. And we'll let Max take out Khamenei. We can't film that part, though, people, may tie it to the SEAL attack on al-Zawahiri. We'll strike tonight around mid-night.

Around mid-night Zakkova and his men drove up to the front gate of Khamenei's mansion in their Quds vehicle. There were two guards manning the gate.

"Good evening, gentlemen. I have an order here from President Ahmadinejad to inspect the security system of Grand Ayatollah Sayyed Ali Hosseini Khamenei's house. Through our intelligence network we have received a credible threat against the life of the Grand Ayatollah Sayyed Ali Hosseini Khamenei. We're here to check the security systems to make sure no one can enter the Grand Ayatollah Sayyed Ali Hosseini Khamenei's house that is unauthorized," said Zakkova in perfect Farsi.

The guards stood at attention and saluted the four star Quds general and were in awe of him because of his immense size and the four stars on his label.

"Good evening, general. May we see the directive from President Ahmadinejad?" asked the head guard.

Zakkova pulled out the directive and gave it to the guards.

"This seems to be all in order. We welcome you to inspect our security procedures. I think you will be impressed with our procedures."

"Okay, then please open the gate so we can drive to the front door."

The guard opened the gate and Zakkova and the men started to drive through it. Zakkova stopped the vehicle right at the inside of the gate entrance. Both guards came up to the driver's side window to see what else Zakkova wanted.

"Is everything alright? Do you need anything from us?"

"Everything is just fine," said Zakkova as he pulled out is modified SIG P226 suppressed pistol and put two bullets into the head of each guard killing them instantly.

"Shalom, hide those guard's bodies and stay at the gate. Radio me if Khamenei has any visitors coming."

Zakkova drove the vehicle up to the front door of the mansion and the men exited the vehicle.

"Don, patrol the grounds and take out any guards that may be outside guarding the house," directed Zakkova.

Zakkova and the two other men went to the front door of the mansion. It was a large heavy double door but there were no security devices that had to be shut down so they could enter. The front door was unlocked. Zakkova opened the door and rolled in two security camera jammers. They then entered the mansion and started a room by room search to clear the first floor of any guards. They found two men in the kitchen that Mark quickly dispatched with his suppressed HK 53 submachine gun. He tripled tapped each guard in the head and they died instantly. There were two more guards in the living room drinking tea. When they saw Zakkova they immediately stood up and saluted him. Zakkova returned their salute with two rounds each from his SIG P226. They went down a hallway where there were six rooms with the doors shut. These had to be bedrooms and one room was undoubtedly the security station.

Zakkova opened the first door on the left and found a man in bed snoring. He immediately shot him in the head. The first door on the right was also a bedroom but no one was in it. The second door on the left was a bedroom with a man and a woman sleeping in the bed. Zakkova riddled these bodies with bullets from his SIG P266.

The second door on the right was locked. Zakkova figured this was the security room and probably manned by at least four guards. He put his infrared goggles on the door to determine how the men in the room were situated. The goggles showed two men on the left side of the room and two men on the right side. Zakkova lightly tapped on the door with the barrel of his HK 53.

"Who is it and what do you want?" asked one of the guards.

"I am general Komeni of the Quds force. I have been ordered by President Ahmadinejad to check all security procedures here. Please open the door."

A moment later they heard a series of locks being disengaged and then the door opened. Zakkova and Mark walked in and calmly shot all four men before they had time to respond.

They checked the third door on the left and found it unlocked. They opened the door and found two men sleeping in cots. Mark triple tapped each of them in the head with his automatic weapon.

There was no one in the third room on the right so they made their way upstairs to where Khamenei was.

There was one guard in the hallway in front of a big double door. This must be Khamenei's private room thought Zakkova. He immediately shot the guard in the head putting him out of commission. Zakkova and his men moved down the hallway and opened the unlocked door.

They found President Ahmadinejad propped up in bed watching child pornography on a big wide screen TV. There was no one else in the room.

"Well look at this, another devout Muslim watching child porn. You're the second one so far that I've found watching this trash. You must be taking after our damnable prophet Mohammad who was a pedophile and a mass murderer" said Zakkova.

"Who are you? Why are you here? And how dare you blaspheme our holy prophet," yelled the Ayatollah.

"I was sent by Allah to send you to paradise, although I think you'll go to hell instead. Your prophet was pathetic. How many innocent men, women and children did Jesus kill? How many thirteen-year-olds did Jesus screw? That's right, unlike your prophet none. And you pray to this abdominal piece of shit. And I got some news for you. The twelfth Imam, al Mahdi, is never coming to kill all of the Jews and infidels. What a crock of shit that is."

"You are crazy to talk about Mohammad that way. You will surely rot in hell for that. Mohammad only killed the unbelievers who deserved to die for practicing their pagan religions. Now what do you want?"

"I want a little private time between you and my friend Max."

Zakkova removed the pack from his back and opened it up and withdrew Max, the king cobra. Zakkova showed Max his target. It took two seconds for Max to crawl on top of Khamenei's lap and Khamenei started screaming when he saw and felt the huge cobra on his lap. Max stood up to eye level with Khamenei and then coiled up and let out a loud hiss. Max was ready to strike.

"Max, strike heart," commanded Zakkova.

Max struck immediately ripping Khamenei's chest open and tearing out his aorta with his razor sharp long fangs. Khamenei screamed in pain when Max did this but it was the last sound he would make. He was dead within ten seconds. Zakkova then shot Khamenei in the head to confuse his cause of death.

"Good boy, Max. Come here for your treat," said Zakkova.

Max quickly crawled back to Zakkova with anticipation in his eyes. He wasn't disappointed. Zakkova pulled out a large chunk of milk chocolate and fed it to Max. Max devoured it quickly.

"Okay, buddy, good job. Back in the pack, we need to get out of here. Did you get a video of all of that, Mark?"

"Yes, Zakkova, I got it all."

Max crawled back into the pack and Zakkova threw it over his shoulder.

Zakkova and Mark left Khamenei's room and went back downstairs and collected Sammy. They all walked out the front door. Zakkova keyed his radio and told Don to meet them at the front gate. Zakkova, Mark and Sammy drove the Quds vehicle back to the front gate. Don soon appeared and got into the Quds vehicle. Shalom also got into the Quds vehicle with Zakkova and the others and they drove off.

They drove to a deserted industrial complex not far from Ahmadinejad's mansion and exited the vehicle.

"Good job, men. That went well. One down and one more to go. Starting tomorrow we need to recon Ahmadinejad and determine what his movements are. After Khamenei's assassination, I'm sure they'll put extra security on Ahmadinejad. We need to find the weak spot in their security detail.

Chapter 10

The men spent the week watching Ahmadinejad's movements both at his mansion and at his office in the Supreme Palace. As Zakkova predicted, there was a heavy security detail assigned to Ahmadinejad. There were around twenty guards stationed at his mansion and even more at the palace.

"We can't take out Ahmadinejad at his mansion. There are just too many guards there and even more at the palace. He has been leaving his office at about 8:00 PM every evening and going home. It's a three car convoy. Two cars are carrying six Quds forces and the car with Ahmadinejad in it has five Quds in it. Ahmadinejad's limo is in the middle of the convoy. Our best bet is to take out the entire convoy and kill everyone in the limos. I have a special weapon that will do the job. Let's be ready tonight to follow the convoy and put the hurt on Ahmadinejad. They'll think of nothing if a Quds vehicle is following them. They'll just think that it is extra security.

The men waited until night parked two blocks from the palace. They had a clear view of the palace gates and could see who was leaving or arriving. Zakkova had slit an opening in the canvas top of the Quds vehicle. He used the opening to stand up and mount his secret weapon.

"What kind of weapon is that, Zakkova?" asked Sammy.

"Ah, this is really cool. My friend Jake and Inverse Technologies gave me this. It's not even operational yet. It's a mini electromagnetic rail gun. It fires these rockets. The rockets are ejected by a magnetic field that is activated down the barrel of the gun. It has one hundred times the explosive energy of an RPG and four times the range. One hit from this gun will completely destroy a car. There will be literally nothing left of it after the rocket hits it.

"Wow! I can't wait to see that in action."

On schedule Ahmadinejad and his security detail pulled out of the palace and headed toward Ahmadinejad's mansion. Zakkova and the team quickly started the engine of the Quds vehicle and drove off towards Ahmadinejad's convoy. Within minutes they pulled right behind the third limo in the convoy.

"We'll wait until they reach the private road that leads up to Ahmadinejad's mansion. That's where we'll strike. They'll be no witnesses there," says Zakkova.

When the convoy turned into the private road, Zakkova had Sammy back off about two hundred yards so his vehicle would not be caught in the explosion of the last limo in the convoy. As Sammy drove the Quds vehicle, Zakkova stood up in the bed of the truck and pulled his rail gun up through the hole in the canvas top. His laser sighted the third limo in the convoy and he fired the rail gun at it. The rocket obliterated the third limo. There was virtually nothing left of it, except for a burning hunk of metal. The explosion caused those driving the other two limos to stop to see what had happened. They made perfect targets for Zakkova's rail gun. Zakkova quickly reloaded the rail gun and re-aimed it on the second limo containing Ahmadinejad. He fired the gun and blew the limo to pieces. Zakkova reloaded again and fired at the first limo in the convoy destroying it instantly. They pulled up to where the second limo was and got out and inspected the damage. There was nothing left of the limo. They spotted severed limbs and blood pools where the blast occurred.

"Well, I think that's the end of Ahmadinejad. Sammy upload the video of this attack to Langley. Now let's get the hell out of Iran."

Chapter 11

Within two hours the video of Khamenei's and Ahmadinejad's assassinations hit the airwaves with a narrative by the Arab accented speaker.

Hello peaceful people of the world. This is Mission for World Peace. Tonight our operatives assassinated two very evil men, Grand Ayatollah Sayyed Ali Hosseini Khamenei and President Ahmadinejad of Iran. These men were sponsoring terrorism around the world and developing a nuclear weapon that they vowed to use against Israel and the United States. The world is a much safer place now without these two men. People of Iran, I encourage you to now take control of your destinies. The peaceful countries of the world will be your friends and are ready to assist you in any way to take control of your government. May God bless you all.

"Damn, David, Zakkova pulled it off again. I just watched the video. It was fascinating. I hope the opposition party in Iran takes Zakkova's advice and stages a coup," said President Daniels.

"Zakkova is an incredible force to reckon with. I don't believe anyone could outsmart him or defeat him in battle. The video is having its intended effect. Iranians are pouring into the streets to protest their government and the Ayatollahs according to my sources. We will send in some CIA operatives along with a Delta Force team to help stir up the trouble there for Iran's government. I think the Quds forces will be called in to quell the protests. They'll start killing people right away. That's why I want a Delta Force in there. They'll be able to put the squeeze on the Quds forces and stop them from killing the protesters."

"Okay, that's good David. Keep me apprised of the developments over there. This could be a big win for us."

Zakkova and his men made their way back to the Iraqi border where they entered Iran. Zakkova radioed ahead so the MC-130H was waiting for them when they arrived. The MC-130H flew the men back to Bagdad airport. The men offloaded the MC-130H with all of their gear and loaded onto Zakkova's Gulfstream G650. Zakkova flew each man back to his home and then flew to D.C. to debrief the president.

When Zakkova entered the Oval Office he was greeted with a hero's welcome by the president and his cabinet members.

"Congratulations Zakkova. You did it again. The videos were amazing. You took down the whole mountain at Qom. That will set Iran's nuclear ambitions back by years. And you assassinated Grand Ayatollah Sayyed Ali Hosseini Khamenei and President Ahmadinejad. That had its desired effect we wanted. The young people and opposition leaders are taking to the streets and protesting an overthrow of the government. We're not going to make the same mistake as the previous administration and just sit back and watch. David is sending teams of CIA operatives and Delta Force in to help bring about a regime change," said the president.

"You're welcome Mr. President. I'm glad I could do something to make a difference. Sending help to the opposition forces is a wise thing to do. I believe with Khamenei and Ahmadinejad out of the way conditions are ripe for a government change that will be friendly to the U.S. and the west. Israel should sleep better now that we put these forces in motion."

"Zakkova, what was that weapon you used on Ahmadinejad's convoy?" asked General Sherman.

"Oh, you will need to talk to my buddy Jake at Inverse Technologies. He developed it and let me test it out on this mission. It is a mini electromagnetic rail gun that fires rockets at supersonic speeds. The rockets have one hundred times the explosive force of an RPG and four times the range. The one I used is the only one in existence. It's a very deadly weapon that performed flawlessly. You need to give Jake a contract to make these for all of your forces. It's really a game changer."

"Zakkova, Iran claims you killed over three hundred civilians at Qom. Is this true?" asked Jane Cochran the Secretary of State.

"Well, I didn't exactly do a head count but that's probably in the ball park. There were thirty underground floors and there were undoubtedly many people working on each floor."

"Wasn't there a way to minimize the civilian casualties?"

"What was I supposed to do, evacuate thirty floors of people before I set off my bomb?"

"You're so cavalier about taking so many lives. Doesn't that bother you?"

"Not at all Madame Secretary, I sleep well at night. Look, these people were manufacturing weapons of mass destruction that they vowed to use against us and Israel. There were no innocent people in that facility. They deserved to die. If you can't take the bloodshed from these operations, then I suggest you don't attend the meetings."

"Zakkova is right. There would have been no way to prevent civilian casualties and destroy the Qom facility. This is just collateral damage that could not be avoided," said General Sherman.

This shut the Secretary of State up but she gave the general and Zakkova a harsh look.

"Hey, Zakkova, did Max get to have some fun on this mission?" asked CIA Director David Peters.

"Yeah, he sure did. He actually killed Grand Ayatollah Sayyed Ali Hosseini Khamenei. He ripped his aorta out of his chest. I had to cut this from the video because after al-Zawahiri's death people may have thought SEAL Team 6 was striking again. I put a bullet in his forehead to confuse the cause of death. Here's an unedited version of the video with Max in it," said Zakkova as he took out a DVD and gave it to the president.

"Once again, Zakkova, we appreciate your exploits. You have done a great service to your country and to the world. You should be proud. The other half of your payment has already been wired to your account," said the president.

"It was my pleasure Mr. President. I'm always glad to help our great nation in any way possible. I look forward to my next mission."

"We'll have something for you pretty soon. It will be an important mission that could change the dynamics of the Middle East."

"I'll be ready when you are," said Zakkova as he stood up to shake everyone's hand except for Secretary of State Jane Cochran who refused to offer her hand.

Chapter 12

Zakkova made his way back to Carmel in his Gulfstream jet. He radioed all of the men on the last mission to tell them the final payments had been wired into their accounts. They were all pleased to hear this and each man told Zakkova they would be happy to accompany him on any further missions.

By the time Zakkova arrived home he was exhausted. The high amount adrenaline from the mission was wearing off. He went to his bedroom and took off his clothes and fell into bed and immediately fell asleep. Max hopped up and curled himself up between Zakkova's legs and went to sleep, too.

Zakkova slept through the night and was awoken early in the morning by his motion detector alarms at the front gate. He looked at his security monitor and saw Clyde and a few of his bikers. Zakkova pushed the button to open the gate and let Clyde and his men in.

Zakkova put on some black draw string pants and then he and Max went outside to meet Clyde.

"Clyde, my man, what's up?" asked Zakkova.

"We have a problem that maybe you can help us with. The Aztecs have started running guns and are moving their drug trade into Carmel. They killed two of my best men who came in contact with them when they were offloading meth and cocaine in Carmel to their distributors. We had an agreement with the Aztecs that we would be the only gun runners on the west coast and that they would keep their drug trade out of Carmel. I'm in quite a bind now because I promised the Sheriff that I would keep illegal drugs out of Carmel. The Aztecs broke their agreement with me and like I said killed two of my men. I can't let them get away with this. I need to strike back. Can you help me do this?"

"I'm sorry to hear about your two men. Breaking agreements is bad business and causes wars. Bringing their drug trade into Carmel cannot stand. What do you have in mind? If you just want to send them a message you can probably handle that on your own. If you want to annihilate them, then I can help you."

"They're growing too powerful and taking my gun running business away. After what they did to my men I want to annihilate them."

"Okay, we can do that. Where do they hang out? Where's their clubhouse?"

"Their clubhouse is a bar called the Isabella. It's about twenty miles north of here. I can give you the address so that you can plug it into your GPS."

"That'll do. Let me go there tonight and do some recon and then tomorrow night I'll meet with you and your men to go over a plan of action."

"That would be wonderful, Zakkova. I can't wait to see what you come up with. I'll see you tomorrow night then."

"Okay, guys, don't worry we'll take care of these Aztecs. There will be nothing left of them when we're done."

That night Zakkova took off on his motorcycle for the Isabella. It took about thirty minutes to get there. When he arrived, he saw over one hundred bikes parked out front. The Aztecs would be a force to be reckoned with. Zakkova pulled into the parking lot and dismounted is motorcycle. There was no one outside so he walked around the bar to get a layout of it and to determine how many exits and windows there were. After he was satisfied with that observation he entered the Isabella and walked up to the bar to order a beer. Everyone grew silent when Zakkova walked in. They had never seen such a tall and powerful looking man like Zakkova before. Zakkova glanced around to get a picture of what the inside looked like. It was mostly a large room with tables and booths all around it. When Zakkova ordered his beer, the bartender hesitated but then poured him a draft. A few minutes later a large man walked up to him and introduced himself.

"Hello stranger. My name is Romeo. I am head of the Aztecs. This is a private club. You'll have to leave."

"Well, Romeo, head of the Aztecs, I just ordered a beer and I'll stay here until I finish it."

"Look around, stranger. You're vastly outnumbered. One word from me and my men will toss you out."

In a split second Zakkova grabbed Romeo around the neck with his right hand and lifted him off of the floor. The other men who were watching stood up and started moving toward Zakkova.

"Stop right there or I'll break Romeo's neck," said Zakkova.

The men saw that Zakkova was serious and stopped in their tracks. Romeo was gasping for air and swinging and kicking his legs to break free but Zakkova had a vise like grip around his neck.

"Quit squirming or I'll squeeze harder until I squeeze all of the breath out of you. Now listen closely Romeo, no one tells me what to do especially some low-life drug runner like you. I'm going to finish my beer and then walk out of here. If you or your men get in my way I will kill them."

Zakkova then threw Romeo in the air like a rag doll where he crashed into a table and fell to the floor still gasping for air. It took him about five minutes to regain consciousness and stand up again. He walked back to his booth and his men surrounded him to make sure he was alright.

Zakkova finished his beer in peace and then walked around the bar to get the layout of the inside. There was a hallway on the left that lead to the restroom. The hallway to the right led to the kitchen. Zakkova noticed a rear door at the back of the kitchen. All through with his recon of the bar, Zakkova walked back to the club area and made his way to the front door. There were three large men blocking the doorway. Zakkova removed his EK combat knife from its sheath and put it behind his back. He walked up to the man in the middle who made no effort to move. As quick as lightening, Zakkova brought his knife around and threw a forward and then a back slash to man's neck cutting his throat from ear to ear. Zakkova then threw a straight thrust into the man's heart on the left killing him instantly. The man on the right regained his composure and threw a wild right hook at Zakkova's jaw. Zakkova blocked the right hook and then stabbed the man in the throat pushing his blade all the way to the hilt. The man collapsed and died holding his throat. Everyone in the bar just stared at Zakkova in disbelief. They had never seen such a display of violence in their lives. Zakkova wiped the blood off of his knife blade on one of the men's shirt and then quickly drew his SIG P226 and pointed it at the other men in the bar in case they had any ideas about shooting him. Zakkova backed out of the bar and headed back to Carmel on his motorcycle.

Zakkova thought there would be some recompense after he killed three of Romeo's men. He wasn't disappointed. He heard the sound of several motorcycles behind. Zakkova could have easily out run these bikes but he decided to have some more fun. Zakkova stopped his bike in the middle of the road facing the way he came from around a sharp turn in the road. He removed his HK 53 submachine gun from his saddle bag and waited. When the first Aztec rounded the curve, Zakkova triple tapped him in the head. His motorcycle crashed to the road blocking part of it. Zakkova then set the HK 53 on full automatic and waited for the Aztecs to come around the turn. When they did, Zakkova opened up on them killing everyone he hit. The road was now completely blocked with wreaked motorcycles. The other Aztecs were going so fast that they did not have time to see the carnage in the road. This caused a chain reaction crash as each Aztec ran over a bike in the road and crashed. Satisfied with his work, Zakkova got back on his bike and continued on towards Carmel. This time there was no one following him.

Chapter 13

Zakkova met with Clyde and his men the following evening to tell them what happened and to lay out his plan to annihilate the Aztecs.

"Hi guys. I had quite an introduction to the Aztecs yesterday evening. I went to their club house-bar to scope out their club and its defenses. It turns out that they consider the Isabella their private bar. When I went inside to determine the layout of the interior and to order a beer Mr. Romeo, their leader, informed me that the Isabella was their private club and that I was not welcomed there. He told me to leave immediately. I told him to fuck off and that I would leave after I finished my beer. He didn't take that so well and we had a little altercation that left Mr. Romeo flat on his ass on the floor. His men started to make a move on me but thought better of it. I then toured the bar to determine how it was laid out and how many exits there were. When I went to leave, Romeo had three of his biggest goons blocking the front door exit. I guess their intention was to do me some harm. I killed all three of them. Then they made their second mistake. They followed me as I made my way back to Carmel. I could have easily left them in the dust with my powerful bike but I decided to have some fun with them. I waited for them to come around a sharp turn in the road and then opened up on them with my HK 53. As the first of the dead bikers crashed his bike on the road this caused a chain reaction pile up. The following bikes were going too fast to see the wreckage in the road to stop in time. They just ran over the downed bikes and crashed hard onto the roadway. The whole road was blocked with downed choppers. Nobody could get through without running over them and crashing too. I estimate that

I killed at least twenty Aztecs. All in all it was a good night," explained Zakkova.

"Wow! You really did some damage Zakkova. Losing twenty men will put a big dent in their arsenal. It should be an easy matter to take out the rest of them and put them out of business," said Clyde.

"That it should, Clyde. I have a plan of attack that I'd like to over with you guys."

"Sure Zakkova, I can't wait to hear what you have in store."

"Here is a diagram of the Isabella that shows in detail how it is laid out and where the exits are," said Zakkova as he passed out the diagrams to each of the men. "We'll need to steal a van and change the plates on it. The van will be our main attack vehicle. We'll also need a pickup truck to back up and protect the van. They'll be two people in the back of the van. Jax will be with me in the back of the van and will be harmed with a Browning 50 caliber machine gun. I'll be harmed with an RPG launcher. John and Dave will cover the rear entrance and mow down anyone who tries to escape with HK 53 submachine guns. Dan and Sam will place twenty kilos of Semtex on each corner of the building and activate the remote detonators on them. Doug and Jim will have five gallons of gasoline that they'll poor over the Aztec's bikes. When you poor the gasoline on the bikes, make sure to unscrew the gas caps on the tanks. Right after you do that, ignite the gasoline. With the gas caps off the tanks, the ignition of the poured gasoline should cause the bike to explode. We'll start the attack with me firing an RPG through the front door. As soon as I do that, Jax will open up with the Browning machine gun. The rounds from this gun will pass right through the wooden siding of the building. You will essentially shred the building with this powerful gun. I will fire three more RPGs into the building. The RPGs along with the Browning machine gun will kill everyone inside the bar. Clyde, you'll be in the pickup truck with Mark. If anyone approaches the bar while we're attacking it, take them out with HK 53s I will give you. This includes any police squad cars that may show up after the RPG explosions. Doug, you'll be driving the van to Isabella with Mike. We'll all be wired for com so we can communicate with each other. After I fire off the RPGs, I will radio John and Dave. When you hear from me, quickly run back to the front of the bar and hop into the van. After the bikes are ignited and we have destroyed the interior of the bar, we'll make our exfiltration. We'll stop about two hundred yards from the bar and set off the Semtex charges. The Semtex will obliterate what's left standing of the bar. There will be nothing left standing afterwards. I have found a rough trail off of the main highway about midway from the bar to Carmel. Before we attack, we'll leave our bikes in the woods at this turn off. After the attack, there will likely be road blocks set up to check vehicles for weapons. We can't be caught in the van full of weapons. So we'll park the van deep in the woods so it can't be found easily. We'll also bury all the weapons off the main trail. Then we hop on our bikes and head back to Carmel. Doug and mike will travel back in the pickup truck. If there's a road block along the way back to Carmel, the police will find no weapons on us and let us pass. Are there any questions or comments men?"

"Where will we get the weapons and Semtex?" asked Jax.

"No worry there. I have all of the weapons and Semtex that we'll need."

"When will we stage this attack?" asked Clyde.

"We need to wait a couple of weeks until the Aztecs recover from my attack on them the other night."

"It sounds like an awesome plan, Zakkova. We will completely destroy the Aztecs and stop them from their gun running and drug trade."

"Yes we will, Clyde. Now listen men, we will all become mass murders after this attack. If anyone has a problem with that, do not feel ashamed to opt out. Now let's put it to a vote. All in favor of the attack on the Aztecs raise your hands."

All of the men raised their hands in favor of the attack.

"Okay, it's unanimous. Now since we have two weeks before we strike, every evening we'll go through a try run of the attack to make sure we'll be able to pull this thing off like clockwork."

Chapter 14

Using the garage's van, every evening the men went through a dry run of the attack. Zakkova was pleased with their progress and felt they were ready for the real thing. Zakkova had the men meet in the club board room.

"Okay, men, we're ready to launch. Everyone has their assignments down pat. John, you're good with electronics and you're an excellent mechanic. Go steal a van today that we can use for our mission. Make sure it nondescript. We don't need anything flashy. A service van would be ideal because the rear compartment would have no seats. We'll all ride our bikes up to the turn off and hide them well in the trees and brush. Dan, you and John follow us up with the van and pick us up. Clyde, steal some license plates and put them on the pickup truck. You'll drive that up to the turn off with Dave. On the way back to Carmel when we get to the turn off Clyde, put your license plates back on the pickup truck and throw the stolen ones away. Its Saturday so I think the Isabella will be packed to the brim tonight. I want to launch the attack around midnight so we'll leave here around 10:00 PM to give us plenty of time to set up. Everyone stay loose and alert today. No drinking. We need clear heads to pull this thing off."

At 10:00 PM the men loaded the stolen van and pickup truck with all of the weapons they would be using against the Aztecs. They made good time to the turn off and ditched their bikes and got into the van and pickup truck. They set off for the Isabella and arrived there are at 11:45 PM. Doug backed the van up to within thirty feet of the front door. John and Dave hopped out of the back of the van and ran around the building to guard the rear entrance. Dan and Sam leapt out of the pickup bed to set the Semtex charges on all four corners of the building. Doug and Jim left the van with their five gallons of gasoline and immediately started pouring it on the Aztec's motorcycles. They remembered to screw off the gas caps like Zakkova told them to do. Zakkova radioed John and Dave to make sure they were in position.

The time had come. Jax opened the rear doors of the service van and mounted his Browning 50 caliber machine gun. Zakkova inserted an RPG into its launcher. He fired his first RPG at the front door. It blew the door away and large sections of the outer wall. Jax immediately started firing the Browning machine gun and was shredding the front of the building with his rounds. Zakkova loaded another RPG into the launcher and aimed for the left side of the building. He blew the façade off the building and killed everyone who was seated at that end of the building. He did the same thing to the right side of the building with the same result. Jax's machine gun was like a machete. It was cutting people down left to right. As Zakkova had predicted, survivors headed to the rear door of the building to escape. John and Dave were having a field day shooting down men and women trying to get out the rear door. While this was going on, Doug and Jim ignited the gasoline they had poured on the Aztec's motorcycles. The bikes started exploding one by one. Zakkova's coup de grace was a final RPG fired directly into the center of the bar. Just then a police patrol car came down the street with its light bar flashing and siren on. Zakkova hopped out of the van with a 50 caliber machine gun and shot the patrol car to pieces. He told the officers to get out of the squad car and drop their guns. They did as he said and then he handcuffed them together and threw them into the back seat of the patrol car. He made them lie down on the floor of the back seat so the Semtex explosions would not harm them.

Zakkova got everyone back into the van and pickup truck and gave the order to exfiltrate. They traveled about two hundred yards from the bar and then pulled over to the side of the road.

"Alright guys, let's finish this off," said Zakkova as he pushed the buttons on the four remote detonators to the Semtex charges. There were four big explosions at the Isabella and nothing was left standing afterwards. The men had killed over two hundred people in their raid.

They made their way down the highway to the secluded turn off point. They made sure no one was coming or going at the turn off point and then they turned off the road and drove up the small trail where their motorcycles were. Zakkova had them stop halfway to the motorcycles and then climbed out of the van with two shovels and two rolls of tarp.

"Let's go off the trail here for a distance and dig a hole for the weapons," commanded Zakkova.

They walked about two hundred yards through heavy brush from the van and pickup truck to a very small clearing. There they dug a hole about six feet deep and ten feet long. After the hole was dug, Zakkova lined it with tarp.

"Go get all the weapons we used tonight and bring them here," ordered Zakkova.

It took them two trips but they retrieved all of the weapons and put them in the tarp lined hole. Zakkova then took another tarp and wrapped it around the weapons so no dirt or water would get on them. They then covered the hole with dirt and placed pine needles and other brush on top of the hole to disguise it. You couldn't tell that there was a hole there after they were done. Zakkova took out his GPS and programmed in the coordinates of the hole so he could easily find it again.

"Nobody come back here for these weapons. They're hot now. The ballistics can easily be matched to them. I'll come back in a couple of weeks and pick them up. They'll be secure with me. Let's go home."

After hiding the van the men got on their bikes and in the pickup truck and waited until the coast was clear before they pulled back onto the highway. About twenty miles from Carmel they ran into a police road block. Since they were on their motorcycles and in the pickup truck with no weapons the officers bid them a good night and let them pass.

When they returned to the garage and the clubhouse, Zakkova asked them all to come to the board room for a debriefing of the mission.

"Congratulations men. Our plan went off flawlessly. Everybody did their job. For all intents and purposes the Aztecs no longer exist. They'll no longer be at cross purposes with your gun running business and their drug trade is shut down in Carmel. Does anyone have any questions about what we did tonight?"

"Yes, Zakkova, since we were the Aztecs main rivals, suspicions will immediately fall on us for the attack. What if the police or FBI comes to question us?" asked Clyde.

"Don't worry about that. We left no evidence. The weapons are buried where no one will find them and the stolen van is well hidden. We all wore gloves and ski masks so our fingerprints are not on anything and if anyone survived they can't give a facial identification of us. If you are questioned, don't panic. Your alibi is that you were up to your Santa Clara chapter to honor a retiring member. Make sure you call your people up there so they will back up your alibis. Unless they can find eyewitnesses or evidence that leads them to us, there is nothing they can do. They can speculate all they want to. We made sure there were no eyewitnesses but even if there were, they can't identify us. We were dressed in black from head to toe. None of our faces were shown. Are there any more questions?"

"This is not a question but a matter of business we want to put forth to you. We have all discussed this and we all want you to join our club to be a Nomad," said Clyde.

"Well, I am much honored that you want me to be a member of your club. But the nature of my business with the government takes me away from home for long stretches at a time. I wouldn't be able to play a major role in the club's business and I don't need the money. How about this: Why don't you make me an honorary member of the club? I would have no vote but I would be available to you should any threat come to the club."

"That is perfect, Zakkova. We would love to have you aboard in any capacity."

"Great, but I want a leather jacket with your patch on it."

"No problem, Zakkova. We'll ask our seamstress to make one up for you, although it will probably take a whole cow's hide worth of leather to make one fit you."

The men all chuckled at this. Zakkova went around and shook each of the men's hands then hopped on his bike and headed home.

Chapter 15

The next morning Zakkova got into his highly modified Mustang Cobra and went into Carmel to get some groceries. In Traders Joe he saw the beautiful tall brunet that he had seen and spoken with once before when he was on his motorcycle. Zakkova never had time to date or start a relationship while he was in the SEALs because he was always on deployment somewhere carrying out a mission. He was bound and determined to change that now that he was retired. He figured if could not find the most beautiful and intelligent woman in the world in Carmel, then there wasn't a woman like that in the world. Zakkova got up his courage and approached the woman.

"Hi beautiful, are you taking in a little shopping today?"

"Well yes, handsome, it's that time of week again. Wait, aren't you the one who passed me on your motorcycle a few days ago?" asked the woman as she just starred in awe at Zakkova with stunning black eyes.

"That was me alright. I commented on your nice ride the Mercedes SL650 convertible. My name is Zakkova Ikanovich. I live in a big estate just north of here. I am fairly new to the area," said Zakkova as he stuck out his huge hand to shake the woman's hand. His hand completely enveloped the woman's hand and he tried not to squeeze too hard.

"My name is Lola Fermante and own the Fermante winery here in Carmel," said Lola with excitement in her tone. She wanted to impress Zakkova with both her beauty and her brains.

"Fermante Winery, I've heard of that. I hear your aged Merlot is one of the best wines on the market. Do they sell it here?"

"Yes, they do. Get the 1965 Merlot. It's the best vintage."

"I will and I'll have it tonight with my special Chilean sea bass filets. Would you care join me, that is if you're not married."

"I would love to join you. Chilean sea bass is my favorite but it's so hard to get anymore. And no, I am not married. I do have an on and off relationship with one man in town but right now we're off again so I am free to anyone I please."

"It's a date then. Come to my house around 7:00 PM. I live about ten miles up highway 5. Watch for a turn-off on your left. It will be a gravel road. That is my driveway to my front gate. The gate is a huge heavy door. Just blow your horn and my security system will identify you and the gate will open. Then drive up the road to the front door," explained Zakkova.

"I think I can find you but leave me your cell phone number just in case I get lost."

Zakkova told her his cell phone number and gave her his address so she could program it into her GPS.

"Alright then, I'll see you at my place around seven this evening."

Zakkova finished his shopping and went home to prepare for this evening. He wanted everything to be perfect for his visitor tonight.

At 7:00 PM Zakkova's security system notified him that someone was at the front gate. He checked the security monitor to make sure it was Lola. It was Lola so he opened the gate and she drove up to his front door. He went out to meet her at her car.

"Welcome to me casa. I hope you had no trouble finding it."

"None at all, I just followed my GPS directions and it brought me right here. My Zakkova, this is some place. The house and grounds are beautiful. And that big front gate was impressive. I don't think a tank could get through it."

"Yeah, that front gate is made out of two foot thick oak panels with a fifteen inch titanium core. Come on in and I will show you the rest of the place."

Lola was dressed in a tight fitting black dress that showed off her amazing figure in some detail. Zakkova was resplendent in a black silk shirt and black sued pants.

Zakkova led her in and took her on a tour of his house. He showed her his security system that really amazed her. They went in the den and she noticed some certificates on the wall over the fire place mantel.

"Oh my god, you were awarded the Medal of Honor and you have PHDs in nuclear physics and computer science from MIT. You're not only very handsome but you're very smart too. What did you receive the Medal of Honor for?"

"I received the Medal of Honor when I was in the U.S. Navy SEALs. I would like to tell you what I received it for but the information is classified,"

Zakkova showed her his fantastic kitchen and then led her outside to show her the grounds.

"What's that long building down there by the water?"

"That is my firing range. Come and I'll show you."

Zakkova and Lola went down to the firing range and went inside. Zakkova turned on the lights so everything was visible.

"You have five ranges if my count is right. What are they all for?"

"The first range is for knife throwing," said Zakkova as he picked up a throwing knife and threw it at the target fifty yards away. The knife stuck dead center into the bull's eye on the target. "The second range is for bow and arrow shooting. The third range is for pistol shooting. The fourth range is for rifle shooting and the fifth range is for sniper shooting. Do you know how to shoot a gun?"

"Yes, I am quite a marksman at it. My father taught me and I've been shooting since I was a teenager."

"Hey, that's great. Come down to the pistol range and you can fire off a few rounds."

Zakkova led Lola to the pistol shooting range and handed her a Berretta M9 nine millimeter pistol. She emptied the clip at the target. Zakkova reeled in the target to see how good she was. About half of the rounds were dead center. Most of the others were in the first circle around the bull's eye. One round was in the second circle.

"That's pretty good shooting. You got half of the rounds in the bull's eye and the others weren't far from it.

Zakkova put a new target up and then put a new magazine in the Berretta. He fired off all fifteen rounds in rapid succession. He reeled the target in and it showed that all fifteen rounds hit dead center of the bull's eye.

"You're amazing, Zakkova. You hit dead center with all of your rounds. Where did you learn to shoot like that?"

"Like I said, I was U.S. Navy SEAL. We practiced for hours a day at shooting various weapons from both hands. I am as accurate with my left hand as I am with my right hand."

Zakkova next took Lola down to his boat house and showed her his forty two foot Cigarette Racing 42X Ducati Edition boat.

"That's a beautiful boat Zakkova. You sure have some nice toys."

"I also have a two hundred foot yacht that is anchored at Carmel's sea front. It is a lovely evening. After dinner we'll take a cruise around the harbor."

Zakkova led her back into the house and set her down at the dining room table. He opened up a bottle of Fermante 1965 Merlot and poured her a glass. He checked the sea bass to make sure it was ready. Everything was ready to eat. Zakkova served Lola a sea bass filet along with grilled asparagus in olive oil and a hickory nut soufflé.

"My god, Zakkova, this is delicious. It's just melting in my mouth. The soufflé is just amazing. You're an expert chef along with everything else. You're just incredible. You also have good taste in wines."

"I'm glad you are enjoying it. The Chilean sea bass is no longer sold in the U.S. It's becoming a very rare fish that's almost extinct from overfishing. But I have a secret source for it so I can get as much as I want. It's very expensive, though."

After dinner Zakkova served some cream filled puffs that were baked with cinnamon sugar on top. Lola devoured ten of these because they were so good.

When they were though eating, Zakkova took Lola down to the boat house. He lowered the Ducati into the water and fired up the 1,100 hundred horse power Mercury racing engines.

The Lake behind Zakkova's house had an inlet to the Pacific Ocean. Zakkova cruised the powerful boat through the lake and inlet into the ocean. It was a beautiful star lit night and provided a very romantic setting. Zakkova had brought another bottle of Merlot with him. They anchored the boat and drank the wine under the star lit sky. They chatted for a couple of hours. They had so much in common that the conversation was easy and natural. They told each other about their lives and shared various intimacies. This was truly a match made in heaven and Zakkova felt very happy that he was finally getting close to a beautiful and intelligent woman.

Zakkova let Lola drive the boat back home. She had a blast gunning the engines and reached a speed of ninety knots with plenty of power left to go faster.

When they got back into the house, they collapsed into each other's arms and kissed each other with great fervor. Zakkova picked Lola up and carried her to the master bedroom. Once there, they started taking each other's clothes off. When they were completely naked they just stared at each other's amazing bodies. They climbed into Zakkova's giant bed and made passionate love for three hours straight. Totally spent from their love making, they fell asleep in each other's arms.

In the middle of the night Lola felt something moving on the bed. She woke up and started screaming.

"Oh my god, Zakkova, there's a huge snake in the bed. He's enormous."

"Calm down, Lola. That is Max my one hundred foot one hundred forty pound King Cobra. He is my constant companion. We love each with all of our hearts. He will do anything I ask him to do. He likes to sleep with me every night to protect me. Max, come say hello to Lola."

Max crawled up Lola's body and coiled up on her chest. He raised his head and hissed softly.

"Ah, Max likes you. When he hisses softly like that he is showing affection. Stroke him lightly on top of his head. He loves that."

With much hesitation Lola started stroking Max on top of his head. Max started hissing louder. He loved what Lola was doing to him.

"Max likes you very much. You now have a friend for life. Max, go to sleep now."

With that command Max moved back between Zakkova's legs and curled up and put his head down softly on Zakkova's knee.

"I don't believe it, a King Cobra for a pet. Who would ever believe that? And he is smart. He does whatever you ask him to do. Where did you get him and how long have you had him?"

"I got Max when he was a baby from a snake handler in India about six years ago. We took to each other right away. I taught him how to react to my commands and took him everywhere I went. We grew closer and closer as time went by to the point that Max will do anything to please me. Max is a real warrior, too. Do you remember the YouTube video about SEAL Team 6 Killing Ayman al-Zawahiri?"

"Yes, I must have watched that twenty times. It was fascinating."

"Well, that was Max who killed al-Zawahiri."

"So Max is a hero, too. This is just absolutely amazing. Does Max have the run of the whole house?"

"Yeah, he sure does. He patrols it and watches for any threats. He also spends a lot of time outside. I have a little snake door in the back door where he can come and go as he pleases."

"What does he eat?"

"I usually feed him whole chickens with nuts and fruits. He really loves bananas but his favorite food is chocolate. He also catches wild game when he is outside and eats that too."

"You have a snake that loves chocolate. Are you sure he's a Max and not a Maxine?"

Zakkova chuckled at that and told Lola that Max was definitely a male. After the Max introduction they fell back to sleep and woke up in the morning madly making love to each other again. After the love making, they took a shower together and got dressed. Zakkova made a hearty breakfast of Denver omelets, sausage and hash brown potatoes. They were so hungry from all of their activities during the night and morning that they ravishly ate breakfast in a few minutes.

"When will I see you again, my love?"

"Why don't we go out for dinner tonight? Give me your address and I will pick you up at about seven this evening."

"That sounds wonderful, Zakkova. I will be thinking about you all day long and waiting in anticipation to see you tonight."

They kissed each other for ten minutes and then Lola left to go home. Zakkova was left thinking that this may be the one. His heart fluttered when he thought about it.

Chapter 16

Zakkova was performing maintenance checks on his security system when the red phone that was the hotline to the president beeped and the red light started flashing. Zakkova answered immediately.

"Good morning Mr. President. How may I help you?" asked Zakkova.

"And a good morning to you, Zakkova. I hope everything is going well for you. We have another mission for you. Can you come to D.C. tomorrow for a meeting?"

"I certainly can. I'll fly the Gulfstream to D.C. today. What time do you want to meet tomorrow?"

"Around 10:00 AM in the Situation Room would be good."

"I'll be there. Make sure you clear Max for entry. I'm taking him with me to keep him out of trouble."

The president laughed at this. "I would love to see Max. I'll tell the Secret Service guards to clear him through."

"Excellent. I'll see you at 10:00 AM tomorrow then."

"I'm looking forward to seeing you again, Zakkova. Have a safe trip."

"Thank you Mr. President."

Zakkova then called Lola to tell her that he would be going out of town tonight and had to cancel their dinner date. "Hello babe. I have some bad news. I have to go to D.C. today to meet the president and then I'll probably be out of country for two weeks. I'll call you while I'm away to say I love you and miss you."

"Oh, Zakkova, I don't know if I can bear two weeks without you. Where are you going?"

"I won't know that until tomorrow. But it will be highly classified so I won't be able to tell you."

"I wish you could tell me what you're doing. I'm sure it would fascinate me. Do try to call me as much as you can."

"I will honey. I'll make it all up to you when I return. We'll do something really special."

"Just being with you is something special, my love. Hurry home and be careful."

"Hopefully this will not take too long and I'll be home sooner than expected. I love you Lola."

"I love you too, Zakkova."

Zakkova got his kit together and set his security system on automatic. He called in his flight plan to the terminal and then headed for the airport. With the high thrust engines on the G650 it would take about two and a half hours to get to D.C.

Zakkova arrived on time and checked into the Hilton. The next morning he went to the White House after eating breakfast. He arrived there at 9:50 AM and was escorted to the Situation Room by Secret Service agents.

When Zakkova entered the room it was full of people. The Vice President, Secretary of State, the directors of the CIA and NSA, the Secretary of Homeland Security and the Joint Chiefs of Staff were all in attendance. Zakkova greeted all of them and then the president walked into the room. They all rose to greet the president.

"Good morning lady and gentlemen. Thank you all for coming here this morning. Zakkova, it is a real pleasure to see you again. How's Max doing?"

"Good morning Mr. President. It's good to see you again too," said Zakkova as he took off his backpack and got Max out. "Go say hello to the president Max." Max quickly climbed the table and went to where the president was seated. He coiled up on the table in front of the president and rose to eye level with the president and softly hissed. The president lightly stroked Max on the head and Max put his head on the president's shoulder. The president was ecstatic by this display of affection.

"Max knows who butters his bread and appreciates you greatly Mr. President," said Zakkova.

"He is a marvelous creature and you are lucky to have him. Okay, let's get started. Roll the video Wayne."

On a large flat panel display on the front wall of the Situation Room the video showed heavy artillery shelling of Homs Syria to destruction.

"This is footage of Syrian forces shelling the city of Homs. They are killing innocent citizens indiscriminately. This has been going on for a couple of months now and hundreds of people have been killed in these attacks. Bashar al-Assad is slaughtering his own people. This next footage shows Syrian forces offloading guns and missiles to Hezbollah and Hamas who are using these weapons against Israel. We believe Syria is obtaining these weapons from Russia and Iran. Our intelligent agents in Syria have also reported that Syria is supplying Hezbollah with chemical and biological weapons that were transferred from Iraq into Syria before we invaded Iraq. Syria is also a major supporter of terrorism throughout the world. They are funneling weapons and currency to various terrorist organizations like al-Qaeda. People this situation is getting out of hand. Assad is trying to consolidate his power in the Middle East to devastating effects. There is a major uprising in Syria against Assad. Even some of his generals are defecting to the opposition. If we can take out Assad we believe the opposition will take control of the government. Our covert CIA agents in Syria have spoken to the leaders of the opposition and have been told that they would welcome U.S. involvement in Syria and would be friendly to the west if they took power. Zakkova, this is where you come in. We need you to assassinate Assad. Can you do this?"

"I can do it but it will be difficult. With the uprising in full bloom, Assad has tripled his security detail and rarely leaves his palace. It will take extraordinary measures to take him out. Some of you may object to my methods but I'll need your full support on this."

"Zakkova, you absolutely have our full support on this and any assets that you may need from us. As far as your methods are concerned, that is your business."

"That is good to hear. I'll need two men to work with me on this. I know who I want and I'll contact them today. General, I'll need the use of a MC-130H for a HALO (high altitude low opening) drop and a Raven for exfiltration. Can you provide these assets?"

"It's no problem, Zakkova. I can provide you with whatever you need. Just let me know when you'll need them," responded the general.

"Thank you, General. I'll spend about a week with my men planning the operation. Then we'll be ready to launch the mission. Once in country we'll spend a week reconning the target. I estimate that within three weeks from today Assad will be in paradise with his seventy-two virgins."

"That would be excellent, Zakkova. Will your normal fee apply for killing a head of state?" asked the president.

"Well, in this case because the target is so hardened it will cost you $75,000,000.

"That's no problem. I'll have half of the funds wired to your account today. Does anyone have any questions for me or Zakkova? No, then this meeting is adjourned. Good luck and God speed, Zakkova."

"Thank you Mr. President. I will not fail you. Assad will be dead in three weeks," said Zakkova as he stood and shook the president's hand.

Chapter 17

Zakkova contacted Don Jacobs the former SAS agent and Sammy Waters the former U.S. Navy SEAL and told them about the mission. He told them the payoff was $75,000,000 split three ways after costs. They would have worked for Zakkova for free so the money was just icing on the cake. They both readily accepted Zakkova's mission.

"Okay guys, I need you to come to my place so we can plan the mission. I promised the president that Assad would be dead within three weeks so we need to get our ducks in a row quickly," says Zakkova.

"I'll be on the first flight out of here," said Don.

"So will I," said Sammy.

"That is good. I'll plan on seeing you both tomorrow."

Zakkova then called his good friend Jake at Inverse Technologies.

"Hi Jake, its Zakkova. How are you doing?"

"Zakkova, it's good to hear from you again. When are you going to join me here? We can come up with some crazy shit together."

"There's nothing I would like better than to come work with you. I know we can invent some cool stuff. But right now I am employed by the president as his personal henchman. He's paying me lots of money to do some fun stuff. Your tax payer dollars at work. Listen, I need your help for my next mission. I need to destroy a big building that takes up two blocks in space. Security is too tight to go in and set explosives. I was thinking about using one of your drones to deliver a warhead to it."

"A drone could certainly do it but the problem with that is that a conventional warhead to take out that size target would be too large and heavy for it."

"Yeah, my thoughts exactly. I was thinking about using a tactical nuclear warhead to do the job."

"Geez, a nuke? That may pose some problems. I know the Air Force has stockpiled numerous two and five kiloton tactical warheads. For your purposes you could probably get the job done with a two kiloton warhead. They are compact and relatively light so they would fit nicely on one of my drones. A two kiloton warhead can completely incinerate a two block area."

"That sounds perfect, Jake. Can you get your hands on one of those?"

"Well, that's the thing. All nuclear weapons are tightly controlled and are well secured. I have a guy, though, in the Air Force that can probably smuggle me one. It will be very expensive, though."

"How much are we talking about?"

"It will probably cost $10,000,000.

"That's no problem. I'll throw in an extra five mil if he can get you the warhead within a week."

"For fifteen million he can probably get me one tomorrow."

"That would be great. What would the fallout from a two kiloton warhead be?"

"At two kilotons the fallout would be minimal and would probably spread about two miles."

"That's perfect. How long will it take you to outfit your drone with the warhead?"

"I estimate about five day's tops."

"Can two men handle the drone? We may have to carry it some distance."

"The drone is light, about one hundred pounds. The warhead will weight around fifty pounds. The drone is collapsible for transportation. It will be in a case that two men can carry easily."

"What's the range of the drone?"

"With a fifty pound warhead the drone could probably fly five hundred miles. What's your target?"

"It's classified but I know you have the highest security clearance. The target is Bashar al-Assad."

"Wow, that's a good one. That bastard needs to die a horrible death."

"Getting blown up by a nuclear warhead should make for a very bad day for him. I'll wire the fifteen million to your account today. Keep me appraised of your progress and let me know if there are any problems obtaining the warhead. If need be I can call in my wild card, but I would hate to have to do that. It would put him in a terrible position."

"I'll get started on it today. With fifteen million to spend I perceive there won't be any problems. I'll stay in contact with you over the whole process."

"You're the man, Jake. I'll look forward to hear how you're doing."

"Okay, Zakkova, don't worry I'll get what you need."

Chapter 18

Don and Sammy arrived at Zakkova's house the next day.

"Hey guys, it's good to see you again," said Zakkova as he gave each man a manly hug.

"This is quite some spread you got here, Zakkova. This must of have set you back a pretty penny," said Don.

"It's really more of a fortress than it is a home. Wait until you see the security system I have in place."

"Yeah, I can't wait to see what you got up your sleeve. Knowing you it's something spectacular."

"I'll show you later but let's first sit down and go over the mission I have planned. I'll get us some coffee first."

The two men and Zakkova set down at the table and Zakkova rolled out a map of Damascus, Syria.

"Since the uprising, Assad rarely leaves the palace and if he does, he has a full platoon of soldiers escorting him as well as his personal security detail. He would be a very hard target to hit out in the open without compromising ourselves," said Zakkova.

"Ain't that the truth? Assad is running scared now and trying to butcher the opposition. I hear some of his generals are so disgusted with his tactics that they have defected to the opposition," said Sammy.

"That's right. He's losing control of his government and his military. The defections just seem to make him more ruthless against the opposition. If we can take Assad out, there's a good chance that a democratic government will be formed that's friendly to the west. We can really do some good here."

"But if he's guarded so well and hardly leaves his palace, how are we going to get him," asked Sammy.

"Ah, that's where my friend Jake at Inverse Technologies comes in. He's going to supply us with a drone armed with a two kiloton nuclear warhead. Two kilotons will flatten the palace and all the structures within two blocks of it."

"My God, a nuclear warhead? How on earth did Jake get his hands on one of those?"

"Jake is very resourceful. He doesn't divulge his sources, though, and I don't ask him. The drone and the warhead will cost us $15,000,000."

"15,000,000 are cheap if it will take down Syria's wretched government. How big is the drone and where will we launch if from?" asked Don.

"Jake says the drone weighs one hundred pounds and the warhead weighs fifty pounds. So it will not be too cumbersome to transport. We'll have an MC-130H fly us to Syria's border in the desert with a Humvee. Jake says the drone has a range of five hundred miles so we can stand off quite away from the target."

"What will the fallout be from a two kiloton nuclear warhead?" asked Sammy.

"Jake says the fallout will be minimal and not spread more than two miles. Of course ground zero will remain hot for a long time. They won't be rebuilding a palace there for a long time."

"When will the drone and the warhead be ready?" asked Don.

"I just talked to Jake this morning and he will have possession of the warhead by tomorrow. He said it will take five days to do the modifications to the drone for the warhead and perform the functional tests. I'll fly up tomorrow evening and get it when it's ready."

"What is the plan on the ground?" asked Don.

"We'll drive the Humvee through the desert to within fifty miles of Damascus. Sammy and I will assemble the drone and activate the warhead. Don, I'll need you to drive the Humvee into Damascus to shoot video of the explosion. I think you can get a good video from the main road to the palace. Stay at least five miles away so you won't be affected by the shockwave or the radiation fallout. After filming the explosion and its aftermath, drive the Humvee back to where Sammy and I are. We'll have a Raven ready to exfiltrate us when we're done. We'll blow up the Humvee so there can be no trace elements that we were here. I have the GPS coordinates for the palace so we'll be able to program these into the drone's guidance system. Jake says there are three ways to detonate the warhead. We can do it with an altimeter, a strike detonator or we can do it manually by radio control. I'm going tell Jake we want to do it manually. The drone has cameras on it so we'll be able to see video of the flight path. When it is about twenty feet above the palace, we'll detonate the warhead for maximum destruction.

"When will we leave?" asked Sammy.

"We'll leave in four days. I'll fly up to Oakland and get the drone and the warhead the day after tomorrow. Then we'll leave two days after that. We'll fly the Gulfstream to Bagdad where we'll meet up with our MC-130H crew."

"I'll go stir crazy waiting to get to Syria," said Don.

"Nah, there's plenty for you to do here. I have a shooting range out back that you can use to hone your shooting skills and Carmel is a wonderful place with lots of beautiful women. You won't get bored."

"Okay, that sounds like fun to me."

"Alright, are we all in agreement on the mission plan?" asked Zakkova.

"I think it is a good plan. It will be fun to actually nuke something," said Sammy.

"I'm with Sammy. They pay is good and the mission is challenging."

"We're getting paid $75,000,000 for this job. Subtracting the cost of the drone and the warhead from that leaves $60,000,000 to split three ways. So that's $20,000,000 apiece. I've been given a down payment so I'll wire your share of that into your accounts today. We get the balance when we complete the mission."

Chapter 19

Zakkova and the men arrived in Bagdad at about 10:00 AM in the morning. They weren't tired so they would do the mission that day. Zakkova checked with the MC-130H and the Raven crews and they said they would be able to launch within an hour. The Humvee was already secured in the cargo area of the aircraft.

After a hearty breakfast, the men loaded their gear and weapons inside the MC-130H. They were all carrying Berretta SC 70/90 assault rifles, a very good weapon for both close in and far out targeting.

The MC-130H took off about noon time. It took ninety minutes to fly to the landing zone at the Iraqi and Syrian border. When they arrived, they immediately disembarked the aircraft in the Humvee and let the MC-130H head back to base.

The men had about a hundred mile drive through the desert to get within fifty miles of Damascus. They made good time and arrived at around 2:30 PM in the afternoon. Zakkova and Sammy unloaded the drone from the Humvee and started assembling it. Don drove on to Damascus and radioed back when he arrived.

"I've just driven by the palace and Assad's limo and security vehicles are there so he must be inside."

"Okay, then the mission is a go for today. Back off five miles and wait for the fireworks," said Zakkova.

"Roger that."

Zakkova and Sammy carefully assembled the drone and warhead. Zakkova loaded the GPS coordinates into the drone's guidance system. He then armed the warhead and set the radio controlled detonator to the on position. When they were done doing that they spooled up the drone's small turbo fan engine. It started immediately and was responsive to the radio controller that Zakkova had in his hands.

The desert was hard packed sand where they were which made for a smooth take off for the drone. Zakkova increased power on the turbo fan engine and released the brake. The droned traveled quickly down the makeshift runway and was airborne within a hundred feet. Zakkova and Sammy watched the drone's flight path on a ruggedized laptop computer.

The drone had a top speed of three hundred miles per hour so it wouldn't take long to reach the palace. About fifteen minutes after launch the drone reached the outer city limits of Damascus. Zakkova had kept the drones altitude low so it could not be picked up by radar.

Zakkova and Sammy watched in fascination as the drone made its way to the palace. When the drone was within two hundred yards of the palace, Zakkova increased the altitude to where it would be twenty feet above the center of the palace when he detonated the warhead. The drone climbed up above the palace and when it was dead center of the palace, Zakkova pushed the detonator button on his controller. There was an enormous explosion that threw flames and debris into the sky. A small mushroom cloud appeared that Zakkova could see fifty miles away from the explosion. He even felt the shockwave from the blast.

"My God, Zakkova, the palace and everything around it is gone. The nuke completely incinerated everything within a two block radius. There is not a wall left standing. The shock wave knocked me flat on my ass," radioed Don.

"That's good to hear Don. Now take some good video of the aftermath and get back here right away."

Don drove at break neck speed to get back to Zakkova and Sammy. It took a while to get through Damascus because it was in chaos after the explosion.

Zakkova had radioed the Raven after the drone launch so it was standing by ready to exfiltrate Zakkova and the men. The Raven picked up the men and flew them back to Bagdad airport where they disembarked and headed for Zakkova's Gulfstream.

Zakkova called Lola to tell her he loved her and was on his way home.

The media was having a frenzy reporting the nuclear explosion in Damascus along with the demise of Bashar al-Assad and his government. When it was reported that a nuclear warhead took down the palace and surrounding buildings this became the number one international story. The media reported that over five hundred people perished in the blast. There was much speculation as to who did it. Because it was a tactical nuclear weapon that was used, suspicion immediately fell on the U.S. and Israel. The Arab world was up in arms. Iran and Russia filed a complaint against the U.S. and Israel at the UN Security Council. Zakkova released their statement to try to take the heat off of the U.S. and Israel.

> *Ladies and gentlemen today the Mission for World Peace launched a nuclear attack on Bashar al-Assad's palace in Damascus, Syria. Let our enemies know that we have scientists and engineers who can develop any type of weapon. The strike against Assad was done with a two kiloton tactical warhead. Although the damage was great the nuclear fallout from the warhead is minimal and will not spread far. Though we regret the loss of life of innocent civilians the loss of life would have been much greater had Assad remained alive. He was butchering his own people and supplying weapons and explosives obtained from Russia and Iran to Hezbollah, Hamas and other terror organizations. He has also supplied Hezbollah with weapons of mass destruction. Assad was sponsoring a terrorist state that was a threat to the world. We view the happenings of today as delivering the Syrian people from a murderous tyrant. They can now form their own democratic government and constitution and become a free and peaceful nation of the world. We are sure that the United States and other western countries will be ready to lend a helping hand. We from the Mission of World Peace send our thoughts and prayers to Syria and all of the free and peaceful nations of the world.*

Because of the Mission for World Peace's other exploits this statement was lent some credibility, although Russia and Iran contended that this was just a front for U.S. aggressions.

Chapter 20

Zakkova flew Sammy and Don back to their homes and then headed for D.C. to debrief the president.

When Zakkova entered the Oval Office he got a chilly reception from all those in attendance.

"Damn Zakkova, you used a nuclear weapon to take out Assad. What were you thinking and where did you get such a weapon?" asked the president.

"I was thinking I had a job to do and I had to be successful at it. Assad was a hardened target. Our recon of him revealed that he rarely left his palace and the times he did, he was accompanied by a platoon of soldiers and his security detail. There was no way to isolate him to assassinate him. The palace was so well guarded that it was impossible to infiltrate it to plant conventional explosives. Plus, conventional weapons would have been too big and weighed too much to deliver. You would have had to launch a continued air strike against the palace to take it down. A few Hellfire missiles would not have done the job. You would have had to use heavy bombers. The warhead we used weighed all of fifty pounds. It was integrated into a RVIII drone that weighed only one hundred pounds. As to where I got the warhead, I don't divulge my sources," responded Zakkova.

"You are menace and a mass murderer, Zakkova. All fingers are pointing at us. What are we going to tell the UN Security Council?" shouted the Secretary of State.

"I take exception to your betrayal of me, Madam Secretary. I am a man who loves his country and is willing to do anything to remove evil from the world. As far as the UN Security Council goes, you just keep denying any involvement in it. We have released a video from Mission for World Peace taking responsibility for the attack. We wiped out the complete Syrian government who were complicit in supplying Hezbollah with weapons of mass destruction. They all deserved to die."

"Zakkova, what you did was over the top. I am going to have our inventory of two kiloton nuclear warheads checked and if one is missing, I'm going to have the Attorney General charge you with grand theft," said General Sherman.

"Don't throw idle threats at me general. This mission was approved by the president and you. You can't charge me with anything. You hired me to do your dirty work. The fact that you don't like my methods is immaterial. Mr. President, I won't stand for this inquisition. Pay me the balance of the $75,000,000 fee and we'll end our relationship right now," stated Zakkova.

"Hold on Zakkova. I am not taken aback by how you accomplished your mission like my colleagues. You effectively destroyed the Syrian government since offices for all of their government officials were located in the palace. That is a good thing for Syria and for us. I don't want to end our relationship. We need you, Zakkova. I apologize on behalf of my cabinet members. All I ask is that you let me know in advance if you are going to use a weapon of mass destruction. I won't disallow you to do this if there is no other way. I just want to know ahead of time," said the president.

"That's fair Mr. President. The next time and hopefully there will not be a next time, I will inform you in advance if I plan to use a weapon of mass destruction. I would like to keep our relationship intact. We are having a real good impact across the globe.

"You can't be serious Mr. President. You're going to let this thug continue to murder people?" said Jane Cochran the Secretary of State.

"That's enough out of you Jane. If you don't like what we're doing, then you can give me your letter of resignation."

That shocked the Secretary and she just sat there and pouted.

"Zakkova, I will have another mission for you soon that I know will not require a nuclear warhead."

"I will be looking forward to it Mr. President. It's always a pleasure and an honor to serve you. Just contact me and I will fly immediately to D.C. for a briefing," said Zakkova as he stood and shook the president's hand. He didn't bother shaking the hands of the other people.

Chapter 21

As soon as Zakkova returned to Carmel he called Lola.

"Lola, my love, how are you?"

"I'm doing great, darling, other than missing the hell out of you."

"I've missed you too, babe. How about we go on a little trip together? My buddy Sammy owns a beautiful lodge in Jackson Hole, Wyoming. He's throwing a retirement party for one of our SEAL buddies. All of my ex-SEAL comrades and other friends will be there. It will be fun to see them and all of their wives and girlfriends. Plus I get to show you off. All of the men will be jealous. You will really like the ladies. They are beautiful and intelligent like you."

"Oh, Zakkova, that sounds wonderful. When will we leave?"

"I was thinking about tomorrow morning. All of the guests will start arriving today and festivities will start tomorrow."

"Can we catch a flight to Jackson Hole directly out of Carmel?"

"We sure can. I've got that all taken care of."

"I can't wait. Will you come over tonight?"

"I sure will. Expect me around six.

"Okay, I'll be ready for you. Ciao, my dear."

That evening Zakkova went over to Lola's house. They ate an extravagant dinner prepared by Lola's chef. Afterwards they retired to Lola's bedroom and practically ripped off each other's clothes. They made passionate love all through the night.

In the morning they took a shower together and then drank coffee and ate bagels on Lola's back porch by the pool.

"Okay, my dear, I'll go home and pack my gear and pick you up in about an hour and we'll leave for Jackson Hole."

"I'll be ready, sweetie. I am really looking forward to meeting all of your friends. If they are honored to be your friend, they must be fantastic people."

"Good, we'll have lots of fun for a few days."

An hour later Zakkova picked up Lola in his Cobra and they went to the airport. Zakkova pulled up to the private plane entrance gate and showed the guard his ID. He then drove around to front of some very large hangers and pulled into the one that had his Gulfstream G650 in it.

"Well, here's our flight. I think you will be very comfortable on the journey," said Zakkova.

"Oh, my, is that your plane Zakkova? It's magnificent. What kind is it?"

"It's a Gulfstream G650, the largest and fastest Gulfstream made."

"Do you know how to fly it or do you have a crew that flies it?"

"I fly it. I wouldn't trust anyone with this plane. Come on aboard and I'll show you your accommodations."

Zakkova led Lola up the stairs to the Gulfstream and showed her the opulent interior.

"My God, Zakkova, it's beautiful."

"Yes it is. In the back there is a master bedroom with an office and a full bathroom. So if you get sleepy during the flight you can go back there and catch some sleep in the king size bed. The bar is stocked and there are sandwiches and other goodies in the galley kitchen."

Zakkova had already filed his flight plan so they were ready to depart. He had the plane backed out of the hanger and then started the engines. He contacted the control tower and was cleared for takeoff on runway 1.

It was a smooth takeoff and they soon were gaining altitude very fast. They would be flying at 30,000 feet. Lola was sitting in the copilot's seat and was fascinated by all of the instruments and Zakkova's mastery of them.

"Don't you have to have a copilot to fly a plane this big?" asked Lola.

"Technically you do. But I don't need one. I can fly this plane easily myself. I have very advanced avionics in it so most flight functions are done automatically. It's against FAA regulations but I don't care."

"You sure live dangerously."

"Don't be afraid. I know exactly what I am doing."

"I have full and complete confidence in you darling."

"You can stay up here with me or go lounge in the cabin area of the plane. If you want to take a nap, there's the master bedroom all the way back. Help yourself to a drink or a sandwich if you want."

"I think I will go and check out the luxuries on this aircraft. I'll be back in a little while, my darling."

Zakkova and Lola landed at Jackson Hole just after noon. Sammy and his wife, Jill, were there to meet them at the airport.

"Zakkova, my brother, God it's good to see you again," said Sammy as he gave Zakkova a manly hug.

"It's good to see you too, Sammy. I've been looking forward to this trip to see your beautiful lodge again. And may I introduce the lovely Lola Fermante."

"Hi, Lola, it's a pleasure to meet you. Zakkova has told me so much about you," said Sammy as he kissed Lola on the cheek.

"It's a pleasure to meet you, Lola. I am Jill, Sammy's wife. It's so good of you to come. You caught yourself a real winner there with Zakkova," said Jill as she hugged Lola.

"I am so happy to meet you both. Zakkova has told me all kinds of good things about you two and your beautiful lodge resort."

"Well, what do you say we head on there. Most everyone is already there. They'll be happy to see you," said Sammy.

Lola noticed the beautiful countryside as they made their way to the resort. When they arrived there she was very impressed by it all.'

"It's magnificent Sammy and Jill. You are so fortunate to have a lovely paradise like this."

"Thank you, Lola. I think you will enjoy your stay here," said Jill.

As the bell hop unloaded their bags, the four of them made their way into the Grand Room. All of Zakkova's SEAL commandos were there along with some U.S. Army Special Forces men that were good friends with Zakkova. When they saw Zakkova enter the room they all came forward to give him a good welcome. Zakkova introduced Lola to the men and their wives and girlfriends. They all took to Lola immediately. She dazzled them with her big smile and engaging personality.

"Lola Fermante, that sounds familiar. Where have I heard that name before?" asked Betty.

"Well, I own Fermante Winery in Carmel so maybe you've had some of my wine before."

"That's it. I read an article about you in Forbes magazine and I absolutely love your chardonnay. I must drink three bottles a week."

"Yes, the chardonnay is very good and one of our top sellers. You should also try our Pinot Noir. We had a very good grape harvest this year and it really made a difference to our Pinot Noir."

"I'll buy a bottle of that as soon as I get home. It sounds delicious."

Zakkova made his way around the room exchanging old war stories with his fellow warriors. They had all served on special missions with Zakkova in the past when he was a SEAL and at present with his missions from the president. He had all made them multimillionaires from these missions. He walked up to Buck, the retiring Navy SEAL.

"Buck, congratulations on your retirement. It is well deserved. You were an excellent SEAL."

"Thank you, Zakkova, but SEAL Team 6 was never the same after you left. That's one of the reasons why I'm retiring. I put in a good fifteen years so I figured my time was done. I'm worried, though. The only thing I know how to do well is kill people. There's not much of a demand for that skill set out there."

"Don't worry, Buck. I still carry out secret missions for the president. I hire the men here to help me on these missions. We get paid very well by the government. The next one I get I'll give you a call and you can put your skills back to work."

"Gee, thanks Zakkova. I would love to work with you again on some missions. Please keep me in mind."

"I will buck don't worry."

The party moved outside where dinner was being grilled. The men took up a game of touch football while the women played croquet.

When dinner was served they all sat at a big banquet table. They had steaks, chicken, fresh trout, stir fried vegetables and other side dishes. Lola was just talking away to all of the ladies. They were all fascinated by her winery. She invited all of them to come for a visit and a wine tasting excursion.

After dinner they all went into the game room to shoot pool and play ping pong. Zakkova was undefeated playing eight ball and Lola was beating all of the women at ping pong.

Later they all repaired into the living room where they drank port and one hundred year old scotch.

Around midnight the guests went to their rooms to fall asleep. Zakkova and Lola had a beautiful suite with a giant bed in the bedroom.

"This suite is fabulous. The decorating is so well laid out and romantic and it's just huge."

"Yeah, most of the suites are like this one but I believe Sammy set us up in the presidential suite. What do you say we take a shower together and then try out that big bed?"

"Okay, big boy, lead the way."

After their shower they climbed into bed and made furious love three times during the night.

They awoke the next morning and went down to the dining hall for a big hearty breakfast.

"What's on the agenda, Zakkova?"

"I think we'll take a boat out on the lake and do some fly fishing. Do you know how to fly fish?"

"I sure do. Another thing my father taught me and he used to take me on all of his fly fishing trips."

"Hey, that's great. I know of a little secluded spot just offshore a few miles from here. We'll have the chef pack us a picnic basket and we'll stop there for lunch and soak up nature."

"That sounds very romantic. I can't wait to see what nature has to offer."

Zakkova was on his way to see the chef when Sammy stopped him.

"Zakkova, Lola is just fantastic. She is extremely beautiful and so intelligent. I can talk to her about almost any subject and she's an expert on it. She can even talk about combat. She knows the complete warfare history of the United States. The men and women just love her. You're a lucky guy, my friend."

"Thanks, Sammy. I know I'm lucky to have her and I love her with all of my heart. Wait until this evening and I will have a special announcement to make."

"I can't wait to hear what it is. You and Lola have a fun day now."

Zakkova got the picnic basket from the chef and a couple of bottles of wine and then when up to his room to see if Lola was ready to go fly fishing.

"Hey, babe, you ready to go snag a six pound trout."

"I'm ready, Zakkova, let's go test the waters."

Zakkova took the boat out to his favorite fishing spot.

"This is a good spot. I always catch a stringer full of fish here. Now let me see how you cast your line."

In perfect form Lola cast her line out into the water. As she was reeling it in she got a hit on her line. She let the fish run until he had swallowed the hook and then pulled back on the rod to set the hook. This was a big fish. Lola's rod was almost bent down to the water. She let the fish run again and then reeled the line in again. She did this several times like an expert until the fish was too tired put up a fight. She reeled it all the way in and was rewarded with a big trout.

"Way to go, Lola. That sucker must weigh at least eight pounds."

"Well, he put up good fight. It thought he was going to break my rod there for a minute."

Zakkova then casted his line and got an immediate hit. After fighting the fish for almost twenty minutes he was able to reel it in. It was about a ten pound walleyed bass.

"Wow, Zakkova. That is some fish. Walleyed bass are good eating fish. He'll make a good dinner for someone."

Zakkova and Lola fished for another two hours and between them they had caught ten fish, a good day's take. They were ready for lunch so Zakkova steered the boat to his special secluded place.

"It's beautiful Zakkova. Look at all of the flowers. They're so pretty. How did you find this spot?" asked Lola.

"I've hiked all around the lake and one day I came upon it. I was struck by all of the natural beauty and the flat lush grass in the center of it."

Zakkova and Lola eagerly devoured the sandwiches and cheese and caviar the chef had packed them and quickly drank the first bottle of wine.

"Lola, why don't we partake in a little nature ourselves," said Zakkova as he wrapped his huge arms around her.

"Oh, my dear, you come up with the best suggestions."

Zakkova a Lola made passionate love for around two hours. When they were done Lola rested her head on Zakkova's massive chest.

"Lola, my dear, have you ever felt something deep inside you that you knew was right and true?"

"Yes, there have been a few times in my life when I have felt that."

"Well, I have been feeling it for the last four weeks and I'm ready to tell you what it is."

"Oh, tell me Zakkova. I can't wait to hear it."

"Lola Francesca Fermante would you honor me to be my wife?"

Lola was so moved by this that she broke out in tears.

"Zakkova Tacoma Ikanovich you are the man of my dreams. I want to spend the rest of my life with you and be by your side forever."

"I'll take that as a, yes, then."

"Of course, you big stallion," said Lola as she punched him lightly on the arm.

That evening at dinner in the dining room, Zakkova rose with his glass, tapped it with his knife, and got the attention of all the other guests.

"Ladies and gentlemen, I have some very good news I want to share with you. I have asked the lovely Lola Fermante to take my hand in marriage and she has accepted."

All of the guests stood up and clapped and hooted. They all rushed toward Zakkova and Lola to congratulate them with handshakes, kisses and hugs.

Zakkova and Lola spent another three days at the resort hiking, horseback riding and playing golf. They then bid farewell to everyone and headed back to the airport with Sammy to Zakkova's Gulfstream.

Chapter 22

Zakkova was not home for more than a day when his hotline to the president flashed red. This time it was the president himself.

"Hello Zakkova. I hope all is well with you," said the president.

"Good morning Mr. President. Things could not be better. I asked the love of my life to marry me and she accepted."

"That's wonderful, Zakkova. What is her name?"

"Her name is Lola Fermante and she owns a winery here in Carmel."

"That's a beautiful name. I know you two will be happy together for all time's sake. I hope to meet her soon."

"I'll bring her to D.C. the next time I come and introduce you."

"Then I'll get to meet you very soon. We have another mission for you that strikes pretty close to home. Can you be here tomorrow at 10:00 AM for a briefing?"

"Yes, I can be there. I'll leave here today."

"That's great Zakkova. I'll see you tomorrow and don't forget to bring your lovely fiancé for me to meet."

"We'll both be there. I'll see you tomorrow Mr. President."

Zakkova called Lola to tell her about his trip to D.C. and if she came, who she would get to meet.

"Hello, my love. I have something special for you. How would you like to personally meet the President of the United States?"

"Oh my, I would be honored to meet him. I am a big fan of our president."

"I thought so. But we have leave for D.C. today. Can you put things on autopilot at the winery and come with me?"

"Of course I can. When will you pick me up?"

"I'll pick you up around 4:00 PM and we'll go get the Gulfstream ready for travel."

"I'll be waiting in anticipation."

When Zakkova arrived at the Oval Office the next day all of the players were there, the president, vice president, the Secretary of State, directors of the CIA and NSA, the head of Homeland Security and the Joint Chiefs of Staff.

"Welcome Zakkova. I appreciate that you could make it here on such short notice," said the president.

"That's the advantage of owning your own jet. I can get here at almost a minute's notice."

"Zakkova, I am sure you are aware of what's happening on our southern border. The Mexican drug cartels are getting bigger and bolder. They are pushing illegal drugs and weapons across our border with almost impunity. The violence of these cartels is becoming a real threat to us. Just recently they killed two of our border control agents and one civilian. The infighting amongst the cartels is escalating and adding to the violence we are experiencing at our borders. We need to send a loud message to them that we will no longer tolerate their drug and weapons running and especially their violence. We want you to take out the Sinaloa cartel and their leader Joaquin "Chapo" Guyman. This is the largest cartel and the most dangerous one. If we can take them out it will put a big dent in the drugs and weapons smuggling trade and serve as a warning to the other cartels that the same fate awaits them if they continue to operate on our borders and within the U.S."

"You are quite right Mr. President. The situation on the southern borders is becoming untenable. The Sinaloa cartel is ruthless and big. There are probably almost two hundred people running their business. I would need at least twenty men to take out their main headquarters and the price would be $100,000,000."

"For an operation this large, your fee is reasonable. I'll have half of the funds wired into your account today. How soon do you think you can accomplish this mission?"

"Give me a day or two to get the men I need. Then we'll need sat photos of Guyman's compound. We can be in country in about a week. We'll spend three days planning the mission and another two days reconning Guyman's compound and then we'll strike. So I would say we can have this done in two weeks. You'll need to notify and get agreement from the Mexican government that we're going to do this. The last thing I would want is to get into a firefight with the Mexican Federales."

"I have already spoken to President Mendez and he has sanctioned the mission. He said let him know if you need any assistance."

"I think me and my men can handle it. I don't trust the Federales. They have a lot of men on Guyman's payroll. Get me the sat photos before I leave today so I can start planning."

"Keith, get someone working on the sat photos now and get them to Zakkova before he leaves today."

"Yes sir, Mr. President."

"Zakkova, as always this is an off the book mission so if you get caught you're on your own."

"I am aware of that and I accept the risk."

"Okay, good luck and Godspeed Zakkova," said the president as he stood up to shake Zakkova's hand.

"I brought someone who is very excited to meet you, Mr. President."

"You brought Lola? Oh, that's great Zakkova. Bring her in. The rest of you are dismissed."

Zakkova went out into the Oval Office's waiting area and took Lola's hand and walked back into the Oval Office.

"Mr. President, it is my pleasure to present Miss Lola Fermante," said Zakkova as he led Lola up to the president.

"Lola, what a pleasure to meet you. Zakkova told me a lot about you. You own a winery. That's very cool. And I did some research on it and found out that it is very successful offering some of the best wines in the world."

"Thank you, Mr. President. I am so thrilled to meet you. I am your number one fan. I ran a campaign in Carmel for you the last election."

"Well my thanks to you, Lola. That's makes me happy that you are my number one fan. Now I hear you two are getting married. That is just wonderful. Please invite me and my wife to the wedding."

"Oh Mr. President we would be delighted to invite you to the wedding. We haven't got an exact date yet, but when we do we'll be sure to work it around your schedule."

"You both are exceptional people. I am honored to know both of you. I think you two are the perfect match."

"We better go, dear, the president is a very busy man."

"Goodbye Mr. President. This will go down as one of the most special times in my life."

"Goodbye Zakkova and Lola. Keep in touch. I need strong supporters like you."

Chapter 23

Zakkova spent the rest of the day recruiting the men he would need for the Sinaloa mission. With a $5,000,000 payday it wasn't hard to get the men he needed. They were scheduled to meet at his house the next day. That gave Zakkova a chance to look at the sat photos and come up with a preliminary plan of attack.

The men started arriving at around 8:00 AM the next morning. All of Zakkova's regulars were in attendance, Sammy, Roger, Dave, Don, Doug and fifteen other men that Zakkova trusted and who were proven warriors. Zakkova served all of the men coffee and Danish rolls and then got down to business.

"Gentlemen, thank you all for coming. Our mission is to destroy the largest criminal enterprise in the world, the Sinaloa cartel. The cartel has operations spread all over Mexico but their headquarters and main processing facilities are located in Culiacan. It is believed this where Joaquin "Chapo" Guyman, the head of the cartel, resides. He will be the prime target of the operation. I have some sat photos here that purportedly show the cartel's operation is Culiacan. As you can see, there are several structures in the Sinaloa compound. Most of these are used for processing Columbian cocaine, making methamphetamines and packaging marijuana. This big structure here is like a palace. That is where Guyman supposedly lives. Our intel says he rarely leaves the palace and compound because of his numerous enemies from the other Mexican cartels. Our ingress will be by a HALO drop from a C-130 at 4:00 AM in the morning. We'll be dropped about two miles from the compound in some barren desert land. We'll make our way to the compound and stop about three hundred yards from the main gate.

Intel says the gate is guarded by four men. Roger, you'll take these four men out with a sniper rifle. We'll then enter through the main gate. After that, anyone you see shoot them. We must kill everyone in the compound. The estimate is there are about two hundred people in the compound. I'll have the mini rail gun with me so I'll take down all of the structures except for the palace. That should kill most of the residents. I'll need five men to clear the palace out. Do not kill Guyman unless absolutely necessary. Max will kill him for us. The whole operation should take around thirty minutes. For exfiltration we'll steal some vehicles at the compound and drive a straight shot to Tetuan Nuevo. It's almost a straight shot from Culiacan. We take 280 to 30 and 30 straight to Tetuan Nuevo. I'll have my yacht at the harbor there and we'll take that all the way back to Carmel. Okay, are there any questions?"

"That is a well laid out plan, Zakkova. But as you said, Sinaloa is spread out over Mexico. How will taking out Culiacan stop the Sinaloa cartel from drug trafficking?" asked Don.

"Good question, Don. The short answer is it won't completely shut down the cartel. The main objective of the mission is to send a message to the other cartels. If they keep running drugs over our border they will suffer the same fate. Taking out Guyman and his lieutenants will throw the Sinaloa cartel into chaos. There will be internal infighting to see who takes over as head of the cartel. This will greatly affect their operations for several months. Indeed, the cartel may not survive it and splinter off into smaller cartels," replied Zakkova.

"Will that rail gun actually destroy a whole building?" asked Dave.

"The rail gun is awesome. It fires missiles that have one hundred times the explosive energy of an RPG and four times the range. I used it very effectively in Iran to take out Ahmadinejad's convoy. I estimate two missiles will completely destroy these buildings. Remember, these are buildings where they process drugs so they're probably constructed from aluminum siding. They'll come down easily."

"Do we really need to kill everyone in the compound? Two hundred is a lot of people?" asked Doug.

"Yes, we need to utterly destroy the whole compound and everyone in it. We'll leave no witnesses. You will mostly be shooting down guards patrolling the grounds. Most of the causalities will come from the destruction of the buildings."

"It's a good plan, Zakkova. I would almost say that twenty of us is overkill but the more the merrier," said Sammy.

"Okay, are there any more questions? Good, we'll leave here at 1300 hours tomorrow. We fly to Tuscan to catch the C-130. I have already made arrangements to have all of our gear and weapons shipped there. It's a big payday, boys, $5,000,000 each. I have already wired half of that amount into your accounts. The balance will be paid upon completion of the mission."

Chapter 24

Zakkova had all of the men at the airport at 1300 hours the next day. They flew Zakkova's Gulfstream to Tuscan to catch the C-130 transport plane. They landed in Tuscan about ninety minutes later.

When they arrived in Tucson, Zakkova checked in with the base commander. Everything was a go. The C-130 would be ready to HALO them that night to within two miles of the Sinaloa cartel's compound. Zakkova took the men to the hanger where their gear and weapons were stored.

"Listen up men. My good friend Jake and Inverse Technologies has offered up a new weapon system he wants us to test." Zakkova picked up a black helmet. "We'll be wearing these helmets. They can withstand a hit from a 50 caliber round. The front shield is bullet proof, too. The shield is a heads up display. While wearing the helmet you can switch the display from NVG to infrared. The display has built in radar. It will show you the movement of targets in a wide area. The system is rigged up to this custom made Berretta assault rifle. There are sensors in the barrel of the rifle that send signals to the heads up display. When a target is lined up with the barrel sites a green light of the target will turn red. Pull the trigger and you'll hit the target. The system also has an automatic feature built in. You can set it on auto and the rifle will fire automatically when the target is in the red zone. This is a good feature if you are facing off against many targets. The rifle can fire fifty rounds per second. The helmet also has a full com system built in so we'll all be in constant communication as the operation unfolds."

"Zakkova, that sounds really cool. But it's new technology. Can we depend on it to work as advertised?" asked Dave.

"Absolutely, I have done extensive testing with it in day time and at night. The system worked without fail. Jake only develops the best stuff. But I want each of you to test it yourselves while its day light and when night falls. I want you to get used to the features and be able to work with it without any problems. Have a couple of guys pose as targets about fifty yards away. Track them with the built in radar and simulate shooting them when the radar trackers turn red. Also, Jake provided me with new combat uniforms. They are black and made out of some kind of Nano scale material. Jake says they're harder than steel and will stop any bullet from penetrating the suit. The best thing about them is that they are light weight so it will be easy to move around in them."

The men practiced with the new helmet system the rest of the day and when it turned dark. They were all impressed with the system and couldn't wait to put it in operation. The fact that the helmet was bullet proof gave them some comfort.

The men boarded the C-130 about 2:00 AM that night. The flight to Culiacan would take about two hours. When the men neared the drop zone, they started gearing up. Each man checked the other man's gear to make sure everything was in order. Zakkova went to each man and placed a four inch by two inch sticker on their chests and backs. These stickers would glow brightly when seen through NVG or infrared light. This would prevent any chance of friendly fire.

When the men reached the drop zone, they lined up at the back of the plane at the rear cargo door. The pilot signaled the load master to open the cargo door. The men started falling out of the plane one by one. They were at 25,000 feet and would not open their parachutes until their altimeters read 5,000 feet. Since they were all dressed in black combat gear and the parachutes were black it was unlikely they would be spotted.

It was a perfect drop. Each man landed a few yards from each other. They quickly unhooked their parachutes and stowed them behind some brush. The two mile walk to Sinaloa's compound went without incidence. When they got within three hundred yards from the front gate, Roger unfolded his Desert Tactical Arms "Stealth Recon Scout" .338 Lapua Magnum sniper rifle with ACC Titan-QD suppressor and L-3-Renegade-320 thermal sight and put it on a tripod on the ground. He screwed on the sound suppressor at the end of the barrel so it would not make much noise. Roger dialed in his targets through the powerful thermal scope. He fired off four shots and the gate guards went down. The men quickly made their way to the front gate.

"Sammy, take your team and clear the palace. Try not to kill Guyman if you can avoid it. You other men disperse and start killing anyone you see. I will set up the rail gun in the middle of the compound and start taking down the buildings. Don, you stay with me and cover me and shoot any survivors that come out of the shelled buildings.

Zakkova moved to the center of the asphalt surface with his rail gun and box of missiles. The biggest building besides the palace was a two story stucco building about twenty yards to Zakkova's right. Zakkova loaded the rail gun with a missile and aimed it at the second story of the building. He fired the rail gun and there was a tremendous explosion when the missile hit it. It completely blew the second floor off of the building. He then loaded the rail gun again and fired it at the first floor of the building. The first floor completely disintegrated when the missile hit it. The noise from the explosions brought out people from the other buildings that provided easy targets for the men. It was pure pandemonium. There were so many people running around that the men just set their rifles on automatic and slowly scanned the barrels from left to right. All of the bullets hit their marks until no one was left standing. Zakkova continued firing the rail gun at the other smaller buildings. It took only one missile to destroy these buildings. Everyone in the buildings was instantly killed. The other Sinaloa guards were picked off one by one by Zakkova's men. All were taken by complete surprise of the attack and Zakkova's men were so well hidden and camouflaged that they couldn't be seen.

"Zakkova, the palace is secured and we have Guyman tied up in his bedroom," radioed Sammy.

"That's great, Sammy. We're about done here so I'll meet you in the palace in about five minutes."

Zakkova folded up the rail gun and took it and the remaining missiles with him to the palace.

"He's right up here, Zakkova. He's been pleading for his life," said Sammy.

"Well, you must have put the fear of God in him. I'll go up and pay my respects."

"Chapo, you don't look so well for the world's number one criminal. My men weren't too rough on you were they?"

"Who are you? Why are you doing this?"

"You don't need to know who I am other than I'm your worst nightmare. The why is easy. You have been spreading your filthy drug trade over the border into the U.S. You also haven't endeared us with your gun running and all of the violence you are causing at the border. It's time to put an end to that."

"But there are other cartels that are doing the same thing."

"Yes there are. But the Sinaloa cartel is the world's largest. We hope to send a warning to the other cartels with the destruction of your cartel."

"I am worth billions. I'll pay you whatever you want to let me go."

"We are already being highly compensated to put an end to your sorry ass."

"How much are you being paid? I will triple your wages."

"Not that it is any of your business but we are being paid $100,000,000."

"I'll give you $500,000,000 to spare my life."

"That's an interesting proposition. Can you wire the funds to my account right now?"

"Yes, I can do that. Just untie me so I can use my laptop to wire the funds."

"Okay, you're on. But don't try anything sneaky or I'll blow your head off."

Zakkova untied Guyman and brought his laptop to him. He wrote down the name of the bank and the account number he wanted the funds wired into. Guyman got busy and started wiring money from several different accounts into Zakkova's account. When he was done Zakkova checked his account to make sure the funds were there and tied Guyman back to a chair.

"That's good Chapo but I think the world would be better off without you."

"But we had a deal! I just transferred $500,000,000 into your account. You can't kill me now."

"Oh, I'm not going to kill you. My good friend Max will have that honor," said Zakkova as he took off his backpack and released Max.

"Max, go meet Mr. Guyman."

Max was in Guyman's lap in two seconds. He uncoiled himself and hissed loudly into Guyman's face. Guyman was terrified.

"That snake is huge. Get it off of me please."

"Sorry Chapo but it's time for you to die. Max, strike throat," Zakkova commanded.

With that command Max ripped out Guyman's throat. He severed the jugular vein and crushed his windpipe. Guyman's last movements were trying to get air into his lungs but no air could get through the crushed windpipe. He was dead in two minutes. Zakkova then shot him between the eyes for good measure.

"Good boy Max. Come and get your reward."

Max quickly crawled back to Zakkova and was waiting in anticipation. Zakkova had a big chunk of milk chocolate waiting for him. Max devoured it with delight and then crawled back into his backpack.

"Okay men let's get out of here. Do we have any vehicles ready to go?" asked Zakkova.

"Yeah, Guyman has three stretched limousines. We should be able to fit all of the men into those and ride in style. I've got the keys to them," said Sammy.

Zakkova radioed all of the men outdoors and told them to come to the palace. When they got there, they loaded themselves into the limos. All three limos left the Sinaloa compound and got on 280 headed to Tetuan Nuevo. They met no resistance on their way.

"Man, this sure as hell beats traveling in a Humvee. We got a stocked bar here and plenty of ice. Let's start celebrating early. I know the guys in the other limos are partaking of this good scotch," said Dave.

"That's okay with me. Just don't get plastered. We need to have a debriefing when we get on my yacht," said Zakkova.

Since it was early morning there wasn't much traffic on the roads and they made good time to Tetuan Nuevo. When they got there they went down to the harbor and quickly found Zakkova's yacht. It was the largest one in the harbor. They boarded the yacht and went directly to the stateroom for the debriefing.

"Alright, men it was a good mission. We accomplished all of our goals and took out the heart of the Sinaloa cartel. Everyone performed flawlessly. Any comments on the weapon system we used?" asked Zakkova.

"Man, that system is awesome. I felt invincible with the bullet proof combat clothes on and with the helmet. I think I took a hit from an AK47 but I hardly felt it," said Doug.

"And the head up display with the radar and aiming sensors was fabulous. I just put it on automatic and moved the gun barrel from left to right and it locked on the targets and automatically fired and hit all of the targets. I must have shot down at least fifty hostiles," said Don.

"I agree. It was so simple to use. Its infrared and NVG modes picked out every target. It was cool to see the red dot on the display when it locked onto a target," said Doug.

"That's good to hear men. The gear is yours to keep. Take good care of it because you'll be using it again on our next mission. Jake will be glad to hear how successful we were using his latest invention. Now I have some very good news. I swindled $500,000,000 out of Guyman before Max killed him. So that's an extra $25,000,000 I'll be wiring to your accounts." The men all shouted with joy when they heard this.

Let's release the video with this script:

> *Ladies and Gentlemen, this is Mission for World Peace. We have destroyed the Sinaloa cartel. This was the largest criminal enterprise in the world. The cartel was running drugs and illegal weapons across the border of the United States. They were extremely violent and are responsible for hundreds of deaths of innocent people. The world will be a safer place without them. All the other Mexican drug cartels are on notice. If you continue your illegal drug and weapons smuggling, we will come for you and destroy you like we did the Sinaloa cartel. Your days are numbered. You will follow in the path of the Sinaloa cartel.*

Chapter 25

Zakkova flew to D.C. after he arrived home to debrief the president on the Sinaloa mission. When he walked into the Oval Office all of the usual players were in attendance.

"Congratulations on a job well done, Zakkova," said the president.

"Thank you Mr. President. The mission went off without a hitch. We completely destroyed the Sinaloa cartel's main base of operation and killed their leader Joaquin "Chapo" Guyman. This should throw the Sinaloa cartel into chaos and severely curtail their drug and weapons running across our border. The other cartels will try to fill the gap left by the destruction of the Sinaloa cartel so I don't think we'll eradicate all of the smuggling and violence at the border. We may need to go in again to take out the other cartels that will rise up and take more control of the drug and weapons trade. But I do think that we sent an important message to these other cartels that they should be careful not to mess with the U.S. government."

"I agree with that, Zakkova. What you did will certainly put a stop to a lot of the ongoing drug and weapons smuggling but it won't eliminate it completely. Let's wait and see what happens and then decide what to do next. We may send you in there again. I looked at the sat photos of the cartel's headquarters you hit. It was utter devastation. You really put the pain to them, Zakkova."

"Given enough time I think we can completely shut down the cartels in Mexico. We should make that our final objective. So I and my men will be ready to go in there again to do some more damage."

"So how many people did you kill this time?" asked the Secretary State Jane Cochran.

"You don't have a need to know that Jane, but there were no innocent people there. These were criminals who were manufacturing illegal drugs and shipping them to our country. These drugs are destroying the fabric of our society. I don't love to kill, Jane, but I do what's necessary to protect our country. I think your liberal roots are showing through." said Zakkova.

"So you say. But I really think you are proud to have all of that blood on your hands. You will address me as Madam Secretary you murderous mercenary."

"Yeah, sure Jane. But I don't take orders from you so keep your mouth shut."

"Mr. President he is being insubordinate. I will not stand for this."

"Okay Jane that is enough from you. You have no business insulting Zakkova. He has performed a great duty for our country that you should be thankful for."

"Mr. President Jane adds no value to these meetings so I suggest you don't invite her to them," said Zakkova.

"That is an outrage. I am the Secretary of State and I have every right to be at these meetings because they affect our foreign relations."

"I will take your suggestion under advisement, Zakkova. Thank you again for the outstanding job. We'll have another mission for you soon that will be very important," said the president.

"I stand ready to perform any mission you might have for me. Just give me a call and I'll come here immediately," said Zakkova as he stood and shook the president's hand.

After Zakkova left the Oval Office Secretary of State Jane Cochran complained again about Zakkova.

"Mr. President that man is out of control. You made a deal with devil."

"Zakkova is the best operative in the world. We are lucky to have him. He is proving invaluable to our national security. He doesn't have the patience for pomp and circumstance and bullshit. You'd be wise to remember that and treat him with respect. You don't want Zakkova as an enemy."

Chapter 26

Zakkova was asleep with Lola and Max when all of the security alarms went off. He woke Lola and took her with him up to his security turret.

"Look, there must be about thirty of them at the front gate. They're going to use Semtex to try to blow down the door. It will not work. The door is made out of two foot thick oak with a fifteen inch titanium core in the middle and there are not hinges. It is gas operated," said Zakkova.

Sure enough the hostiles set Semtex charges at the door to try to blow it down. The explosives had no effect on the door. They then moved to the outer wall and set large charges of Semtex on a section of it.

"They're going to use about five hundred pounds of Semtex on the wall. That will probably blow a hole in it."

The men set off the Semtex at the outer wall and there was a tremendous explosion. It blew a hole about twenty feet wide in the wall. They had two trucks that they drove through the hole in the wall. About twenty men entered on foot.

"Okay, they have breached the outer wall. We'll wait until all of them have entered the property and then set the land mines on automatic."

When all of the men were inside the wall Zakkova hit the auto switch on the land mines. The mines went off left and right and blew up the two trucks and the men on foot.

"See that guy right there? I need one of them alive to interrogate. I am turning off the land mines surrounding him. Look, he's so confused he can't move. That is good. He's the only one left alive. I'm going to retrieve him and bring him in for questioning. I need to find out want organization he belongs to and most importantly who sold me out."

"Zakkova that was awesome. Those mines took out the whole crew. They never knew what hit them," said Lola.

"Yeah, the mines do their job very effectively. Without them I would have to shoot each man and that would take some time. Probably a few would elude me and make it to the house. Now I'm going to go get our guest and interrogate him."

"Can I watch you do that?"

"I don't think you'll want see what I am going to do to him. I am undoubtedly going to have to torture him to get the information I need. It will get pretty brutal. Not for the faint of heart."

"Are you going to kill him?'

"Yes, once I get the information I need he will no longer be of any value to me."

"Okay, I'll wait upstairs then."

"That will be good. I'll need you to keep a watch to make sure no more men show up. If they do, press this button here. That will send an alarm to the room I'll be in and then I'll come quickly back here to take care of the intruders."

Zakkova went downstairs and grabbed his M4 carbine. He went out the front door and aimed his M4 at the feet of the lone man standing. He fired a burst of rounds at the man's feet.

"Throw down your weapons now. Your rifle, pistol and knife need to be on the ground in five seconds or you're dead. Look around you. All of your comrades have been blown to bits. If you want to live, do exactly as I say," Zakkova told the man in perfect Arabic.

The man quickly discarded his rifle, pistol and knife. Zakkova went down to him keeping his M4 aimed squarely at the man's head. When he got to the man he told him to turn around and put his hands behind his back. The man did as Zakkova ordered and Zakkova handcuffed him. He led the man back to the house and took him to the elevator. They went three stories underground on the elevator. Once at the bottom, Zakkova pushed the man down a hallway to a steel door. Zakkova input the security code into the door's keypad and the door slid open. Inside the room was a steel chair bolted to the floor with a desk top in front of it. Zakkova dragged the man over to the chair and made him sit down in it. He then took off the man's handcuffs and locked both of his wrists into wrist cuffs bolted to the top of the desk. The man's arms were now immobile but his hands were uncovered. Zakkova then turned on the video recorder.

"Do you speak English?" Zakkova asked the man. When the man did not answer, Zakkova threw a vicious back hand across the man's face.

"Answer me. Do you speak English?"

"Yes I do," said the man in heavily accented English.

"That is good. Welcome to my little shop of horrors. This interrogation can go easy or it can go hard. If you choose the hard way, you will suffer great pain. I have all of the tools of the trade here. If you are wise you will answer my questions. What is your name?"

"My name is Abdul al-Saede."

"What organization do you belong to?"

The man kept silent and would not answer Zakkova's question. Zakkova went over to a table with a number of sharp scalpels, a bone saw, an acetylene torch, an electric drill and a large framing hammer on it. Zakkova picked up the electric drill with a quarter inch drill bit in it and took it over to the man in the chair.

"I will ask you again. What organization do you belong to?"

The man kept silent. Zakkova took the drill and drilled a hole through the man's right hand. The man screamed out in pain.

"What organization do you belong to?" The man said nothing. Zakkova took the drill and drilled a hole in the man's left hand. He cried out in pain again.

"What organization do you belong to?"

"The Muslim Brotherhood," the man said as he whimpered in pain from the holes in his hands.

"That is good. We are making progress. Next question: Who sold me out?" The man would not answer.

"I asked you again, who sold me out?" No answer.

Zakkova went over to the table and picked up the acetylene torch and lit it.

"Okay now we're in for some real fun. "Who sold me out?" The man still did not answer. Zakkova took the torch and burned off the man's right ear. The man screamed loudly and tried to shake his head away from the flame.

"One more time, who sold me out?" When the man would not answer, Zakkova went back to the table and grabbed the bone saw. He took it over to the man and started sawing off his right hand. This time the pain was too much.

"Jane Cochran sold you out," said the man.

"Our Secretary of State sold me out?"

"Yes, she provided a dossier on you to us. It had all of the personal information about you and the address where you live."

"How much did you pay Cochran for this information?"

"We paid her $5,000,000."

"How were the funds transferred?"

"They went from CAIR (Council on American-Islamic Relations) to a numbered Swiss bank account."

"Who else have you shared this information with?"

"I don't know. That is above my field of knowledge. But I would guess we probably at least gave it to al-Qaeda."

"Thank you for the information. I have no more use for you," said Zakkova as he pulled out his pistol and shot the man between the eyes.

Zakkova went back upstairs to the security turret where Lola was.

"Is everything peaceful here?"

"Yes, no one else has come through the hole in the wall. "Did you get the information you needed?"

"Yes I did. It took a little persuasion but I finally broke the man and he told me what I needed to know."

"That's good. What will you do with information?"

"I will use it to destroy someone's career and possibly life."

"Who is that person?"

"Jane Cochran the Secretary of State. The Muslim Brotherhood paid her $5,000,000 to sell me out."

"Why would the Secretary of State do such a thing?"

"She doesn't like my methods. I think she is a closet liberal."

"Do you have incontrovertible proof that she is behind this?"

"Yes, I have video of the man I brought in here telling me she's the one who sold me out. Now I will get rock solid proof that she did this by chasing the money trail from CAIR to her."

Zakkova went to his laptop and typed in several commands. That put him into CAIR's financial accounting system. He went through the entries and found a $5,000,000 transfer of funds into a Swiss bank account. He printed these pages out. He then hacked into the Swiss bank's computer system and entered the account number that was on

CAIR's financial system. When he brought up the account it showed a recent deposit of $5,000,000 into the account. He clicked on the account profile and it showed the account belonged to Jane Cochran. He printed out all of these pages.

"Now I have everything to bring this bitch down. I'll get on the presidential hotline and request an emergency meeting with the president."

"What do you think will happen when you present this evidence?"

"What she did is treasonous. That is punishable by death. I will want to kill her myself but the president may not let me. At a minimum he will ask her to tender her resignation. But she will have to disappear forever. I can't afford to have her go to trial. If that happens, she may identify me and she would be further compromised and she would tell the court about all of the secret missions I have been doing for the president. We can't let the world know that."

Chapter 27

Zakkova called and set up a meeting with the President for the following day. He asked the President to have the Secretary of State, the Attorney General, the Director of the CIA and the Joint Chiefs of Staff in attendance. He also asked that Max be cleared through for the meeting.

Zakkova flew his Gulfstream into Dulles National Airport the next day. There was a limo waiting there to take him to the White House.

Due to the sensitive nature of the topic, the meeting was held in the president's Situation Room. Everyone Zakkova asked to be in attendance was there.

"Thank you all for meeting with me on such short notice."

"Nonsense Zakkova, you know you have a direct line to me and I will always go out of my way to meet you when you request it," said the president.

"Thank you Mr. President. I wouldn't have called you all together unless it was extremely important. What I have to show you is very disturbing. This all happened yesterday. Let's run the DVD and I'll show you what happened."

Zakkova inserted the DVD into the projector and started it up.

"This is a video of the grounds at my house in Carmel. You can hear the security alarms going off. As you can see there are two trucks and several men at the outer door of the estate. They are going to try to blow down the front door at the outer wall with Semtex. I estimate they set around two hundred pounds of Semtex charges at the door. The explosion was massive but it didn't move the door an inch. That door is made out two feet of solid oak with a fifteen inch titanium core.

You see that they are mystified that the Semtex did not destroy the door. Now you see them setting Semtex charges at the outer wall itself. They're using about five hundred pounds of Semtex this time. An even bigger explosion occurs that blows about a twenty foot wide hole in the wall. After the explosion blows a hole in the wall they drive their trucks through the hole in the wall. About twenty heavily armed men follow on foot. I wait until they are all inside the wall and then set my land mines on automatic. The trucks are blown to pieces and the men on foot on blown up when they step on a mine. You can see that there is one man left standing here in the front of the house. I turned off the land mines surrounding him so I could capture him for questioning. The man is pretty much in shock by the violent and destructive mine explosions. He is essentially paralyzed not knowing where to move. Now you see me go out and confront him. After I told him to lay down his weapons, I went down to him and handcuffed him. I then took him inside my house and down to what I call my little shop of horrors for interrogation. I turned the video and audio feed devices on so you can see and hear the interrogation. Just watch and listen as things unfold.

"My God, you are torturing him. How despicable," said the Secretary of State.

"Regardless of what you've heard or read, Jane, torture is very effective. Just look at all the valuable intel we got from Khalid Sheik Mohammed. That information saved thousands of lives. We didn't get that information by feeding him Tweekies all day long. Everybody has their threshold for pain. When they reach that, their minds will not be able to create falsehoods. They will tell you the truth to avoid more pain and that's the only thing their minds can think of."

As the video rolled, it got to the part where al-Saede tells Zakkova that he belonged to the Muslim Brotherhood and that Secretary of State Jane Cochran sold him out for $5,000,000. All eyes turned to Cochran when the man said this.

"He's lying. I did no such thing. Zakkova is setting me up now. You have to stop him Mr. President. He's a mass murderer and is creating much harm for our country. He tortured this man to say what he wanted him to say. He even murders him at the end of the interrogation," pleaded Cochran.

"What you have done is high treason Cochran. That's punishable by death. But here I have further proof of your complicity. Here are print outs of CAIR's financial system showing a transfer of $5,000,000 to a numbered Swiss bank account. And here are print outs from the Swiss bank's accounting system. It shows a deposit of $5,000,000 into the numbered bank account shown on CAIR's statement. Now when we pull up the profile for that account it shows that it belongs to one Jane Cochran of the United States," said Zakkova as he handed out the print outs of the account profile and CAIR's statement.

"Don't worry about your $5,000,000 Jane. I have it safely stowed away in my account now."

"You can't do that. That is my money obtained through legal means. There's no way you could have transferred it to your account."

"You forget that I have a PHD in computer science from MIT. There is not a computer system in the world that I cannot hack into, even the NSA's. Getting your money into my account was child's play."

"Give me a laptop and I can log into the accounts and show that they are real. You're a traitor Cochran."

"How dare you speak to me that way. You and your stupid snake are a menace."

With that Zakkova took off his backpack and removed Max. "Go say hi to Miss Cochran Max."

It took two seconds for Max to crawl over to Cochran and climb up onto her lap. He rose up eye level with Cochran and hissed loudly.

"Oh God, get this thing off of me," screamed Cochran.

"If I were you I would remain very calm. Any sudden movement might excite Max."

"Jane this proof is indisputable. How could you do such a thing? You betrayed your country. I want your letter of resignation immediately. John, what should we do a about this?" the president asked the Attorney General.

"Well, I think she should be charged with treason and be tried for it."

"With all due respect John, if this goes to trial my identity will be further compromised and the details of our secret missions will become public. That will greatly impede my operations. I think we should just let Max kill her and be done with her," said Zakkova.

"Mr. President he is crazy. You just can't murder me. I demand a trial by jury. Zakkova and his stupid snake are the ones that should be killed for all of the innocent people he killed," said Cochran.

When Cochran said stupid snake, Max struck her on her cheek and bit off a big piece of flesh.

"Oh my God, he bit me. Get this thing off of me," yelled Cochran as blood streamed down her face.

"Max is very intelligent and he does not like to be insulted. One more rude comment like that about him and he will strike to kill," said Zakkova.

"We have a real problem here. I agree with Zakkova that this thing cannot go to trial. Everything will come out in the open about Zakkova's missions and the fact that we hired him to perform them. Any ideas, David?" asked the president.

"Well, we could forge her a new identity and then put in one of our federal maximum security prisons in solitary confinement. No one will find her there."

"You can't do that! I am an American citizen. I demand a trial with a jury of my peers. You can't subjugate the constitution like that," said Cochran.

"On the contrary, you're a national security risk. I have within my powers the means to deal with you as I see fit. Zakkova, are you okay with this idea?" asked the president.

"I would prefer to kill her but that is the second best alternative. As long as she never sees the light of day will be fine with me. The damage has been done. My identity has been compromised and probably every Islamist nut case assassin will come for me. She's put me in great danger."

"Okay, it's settled that's what we'll do. Jane, I want you to type out your letter of resignation right now," said the president as he handed her his laptop.

"I will do no such thing. You can't treat me like this. It's illegal."

"Under my powers it is legal. Look at it this way; if you went to trial everyone would find out that you're a traitor. You'll be a pariah after that. And then you will be convicted and sentenced to death. At least this way you get to live."

"Jane, type out your letter of resignation now or I'll have Max bite you again," said Zakkova.

Under that threat, Cochran typed out her letter of resignation, printed it and signed it.

"John and David get all the details worked out with her identity and make arrangements to put her in our most secure federal prison. Have the Secret Service agents take her down to the jail cell and get her some medical attention for her wound.

"Just so you know, Jane, if for some reason you ever get released from federal prison, I will find you and kill you," said Zakkova.

"General, I need a favor. I have all of the Muslim Brotherhood bodies wrapped in tarp. I would like a C-130 to dump them over the Muslim Brotherhood's main training facility in Egypt. I want to send them a deadly message."

"Sure Zakkova we can do that. I'll have a truck come and pick them up."

"Thank you General."

"Zakkova, I can station some soldiers at your home for protection in case these assholes try to get you again," said the president.

"Thank you Mr. President but as you witnessed I have a very good and lethal security system. I should be okay with that."

"Let me know if you change your mind. I can provide anything that you need."

Chapter 28

Zakkova made Lola another gourmet meal and topped it off with a 1950's vintage wine.

"I am so glad you're home again Zakkova. I miss you so much when you're away. I'm constantly thinking about you."

"Lola, the love of my life, I miss you too when I am gone. The only time I feel really good is when I'm with you."

"I wish I could go with you on your missions. I would love to see you in action."

"Well my missions are pretty bloody affairs. We kill a lot of bad people on them. I don't think you would enjoy seeing that."

"On the contrary, I would love to be part of your team. I think I could do a good job. I hate evil people."

"The missions are very dangerous. Do you really want to risk your life?"

"Yes, I do. I want to feel like I am doing something good for our country like you do. Please train me so I can come with you."

"Okay, you're on. We'll start your training tomorrow. It won't be easy. We'll have to get you in tip top physical shape. Your body must be strong and agile. But think about this. You will be killing people. Are you sure you can do that? Not everyone is cut out for that."

"If they are evil people, I will have no problem killing them. I'll probably take pleasure in it."

"There's nothing pleasurable about killing someone. You're a sociopath if you enjoy it. You kill because it must be done. It's a job that's all."

"I understand. I think I can do it and keep my mind detached from it."

"You just said a very important thing. You must always keep your mind detached from the killing. If you don't, your conscious will get the best of you."

"I can't wait to start training. I can think of nothing better than accompanying you on your missions and being part of the team.

After desert, Zakkova and Lola went to bed and made furious love over and over again. Fully spent, they fell asleep with Max curled up between Zakkova's legs.

At around 3:00 AM Zakkova was awakened by a large explosion.

"Shit, mortars. Come with me. You can be my spotter," said Zakkova.

Zakkova and Lola ran outside to Zakkova's helipad. He had a highly modified Bell Jet Ranger helicopter. The body was covered in kelvar plates and the windscreen was three inches thick. The copter was impervious to high caliber rifle fire and RPGs. It was also heavily armed. It carried four Hellfire air to ground missiles, two Sidewinder air to air missiles and a 50 caliber machine gun in the nose.

They climbed into the copter and lifted off.

"I'm activating the infrared radar system. Any humans and artillery will show up on the display. When they do, the radar will lock on to the target and a Hellfire missile will be launched to destroy them. Keep your eyes on the display and watch for the red dots to show up."

"Okay, I see them. There are four red dots on the display. That must mean there are four mortars aimed at your house."

"Move the cursor over a red dot. Now you are locked on to the first target. Push this button and one of the missiles will launch."

Lola pushed the button and a Hellfire missile was launched. It hit the first mortar to the right and blew it to pieces. It showed up as a large red image on the display. Lola locked on to the second mortar and launched another missile. Same result. She continued until all four mortars were blown up. They flew back to the helipad and landed.

Zakkova and Lola walked the grounds inspecting the damage. Fortunately none of the mortars hit the house. There were, however, four very large craters in the ground. When the mortars hit, they set off the land mines that tripled the explosive power of the mortar.

"I'll have some cleaning up to do tomorrow. I've got to fill in those craters and reinstall the land mines they took out. There probably won't be any human remains or mortar components left after you hit them with the Hellfires. The Hellfire missiles are very powerful so they probably obliterated the mortar stations. It's a shame because I would like nothing better than to drop some Muslim Brotherhood body parts on their main training camp in Egypt. You did a great job handling the Hellfire missile system. Everyone you launched was dead on target."

Chapter 29

Lola had to go to a wineries convention in San Francisco and wasn't scheduled to arrive back home until very late in the evening so she spent the night at her house instead of Zakkova's.

Around 7:00 AM the next morning the alarms went off at Zakkova's front gate door. A quick look at the security monitors showed it was Sheriff Noles. Zakkova opened the huge doors to the estate and let the Sheriff in. Zakkova was waiting for the Sheriff on his front porch.

"Good morning, Sheriff Noles. To what do I owe this pleasure?" asked Zakkova.

"I'm afraid I have some bad news, Zakkova. Lola was murdered last night. Her house keeper found her body this morning."

"Oh my God no! This can't be real. Not Lola. Why would anyone want to kill such a good soul," said Zakkova as he choked up with tears.

"We don't know yet who killed her. They left a note but it appears that it is written in Arabic."

"Take me to her house. I must see the murder scene and I will interpret the note."

"I don't think you want to go there, Zakkova. It is very gruesome. They decapitated her."

"I don't care. Let's go. I will find the people responsible for this."

The Sheriff and Zakkova drove to Lola's house in silence. When they got there, the Sheriff led Zakkova up to Lola's bedroom. There was a full forensics team in the room working the scene. The sheriff took Zakkova into the master bathroom. There sitting on the vanity counter top was Lola's decapitated head. The note was left right beside it.

"Give me some rubber gloves," Zakkova asked the sheriff. With gloves on, Zakkova picked up the note and opened it.

"What does it say, Zakkova?" asked the sheriff.

"It is in Arabic. It says "Blood for Blood MB."

Zakkova was so outraged he threw his huge fist through the wall.

"What does MB stand for?" asked the sheriff.

"It stands for Muslim Brotherhood. I'm going to kill all of them. They will all die at my hands."

"Don't be rash, Zakkova. We'll find out who did this and bring them to justice."

"Don't worry, Sheriff, I will attack their major training camp in Egypt. You won't have to get your hands dirty. Whoever did this is long gone out of the country. You could never find them."

"That would be a major undertaking. Are you sure you can do that and get away with it? If you do that, Muslims throughout the world will be up in arms."

"I don't care about those Muslim pigs. The Muslim Brotherhood is going to pay dearly for this.

Chapter 30

General, this is Zakkova. I need a favor."

"Zakkova, it's good to hear from you. How may I help you?"

"The Muslim Brotherhood killed my fiancé. They decapitated her and left me a nice little note."

"Are you sure it was the Muslim Brotherhood who did this?"

"Yes, the note was in Arabic and said "Blood for Blood MB." They retaliated for my killing thirty-four of them that attacked my house. They knew they couldn't get to me so they went after Lola. Unfortunately she spent the night at her house last night. I want to take out their major training camp in Mukatam Hills near Cairo, Egypt. I will kill every last one of them. I need a HALO jump and then a Raven extraction. There will be twenty of us so we'll need four Ravens for exfiltration. This is strictly a black operation. No one will find out about the HALO drop and the Raven exfiltration. This has to be completely off of the books."

"I'm very sorry about your loss, Zakkova. I hate those Muslim Brotherhood bastards as much as you. I'll provide whatever you need. When will you do this?"

"I need to get the men together and plan the mission. I'll be ready in three days for this mission."

"Okay, I'll get back to you tomorrow and tell you where to meet the MC-130H for the HALO jump."

"This means a lot to me general. I really appreciate your help. I promise that no one will find out about your participation.

"Nonsense, Zakkova. For what you've done for us we owe you big time. Killing your fiancé was a cowardly act. I can have a Delta Force accompany you on this mission if you want."

"Thank you, general, but that won't be necessary. My men and I can handle it. You need to keep your hands clean on this. There will be a major blowback from the Muslims worldwide. They will probably riot in the major European cities and in the U.S."

"Okay, as you say Zakkova. I will provide the MC-130H and the Ravens. If you need anything else, just let me know."

"Thank you, general. I won't forget this."

"God speed Zakkova. Do what you must do. My prayers will be with you."

Chapter 31

Zakkova called Sammy to tell him what happened.

"They decapitated her Sammy. It was gruesome and they left me a calling card. I want to take out their major training camp at Mukatam Hills near Cairo, Egypt. I want to massacre them on their home turf. The pay is $1,000,000. I'll need our regular forces the ones we used for the Sinaloa attack. Can you start contacting them? I'll need all of you here at my house the day after tomorrow to plan the mission."

"Oh God Zakkova, I am so sorry for your loss. Lola was a wonderful person. We all loved her. Forget about the payment. Lola was family. We all take this personally. I'll get on the horn and get the men at your house on time."

"Thank you Sammy for taking this to heart. I'll put the $1,000,000 in a trust fund in case something bad happens. Your family will need the money if you don't come back."

"Nonsense Zakkova, we'll take these bastards out and all of us will return home. I've never been so upset in my life. Killing Lola is a death wish for the Muslim Brotherhood. I will miss her tremendously."

"Thank you Sammy. I love you man. I'll look forward to seeing you the day after tomorrow."

The men arrived at Zakkova's house and all of them were sad and angry over Lola's murder.

"Thanks for coming men. I appreciate you dropping what you were doing and coming here on such short notice. I want to strike back at the Muslim Brotherhood with all of our fury. They'll be no one left standing alive after we're done. General Sherman was kind enough to give us an MC-130H for a HALO jump and some Ravens for exfiltration. The plan will be simple. We'll make the HALO jump about a mile from the training camp around 0300 hours in the morning. We'll take out the guards at the gate with long range sniper fire. When we enter the camp, we'll shoot anything that's moving. Our specially designed helmets will allow us to see everything in the dark. I want at least fifty of them secured with hand cuffs. We'll get those fifty from the barracks where they will be sleeping. We'll line these fifty up in the parade grounds and then execute them. We'll get all of this on video so the world can see what we did. The Ravens will be hovering nearby so after we kill all of these scumbags, we'll exfiltrate on the Ravens. They'll take us to Dubai where we'll fly my Gulfstream back to the states."

"This sounds simple enough Zakkova. This will be a lot of fun killing these assholes. Lola was family. We will avenge her death," said Dave.

"General Sherman said we'll catch the MC-130H at Dubai International Airport. We'll fly the Gulfstream there to catch it. I have all of the weapons we'll need. I'll take you to the armory so you can select what you want to use. My suggestion is that we use the radar operated rifles that we used on the Sinaloa cartel. They worked out very well there. Here are some sat photos of the compound. These two large buildings in the back are most likely the barracks. Sammy, pick your team of five men. You'll get the fifty men I want for the execution from the barracks. Have two men cover while the other three cuff up the men we need. Kill anyone in excess of fifty men. And if any of them start making a lot of noise just shoot them. Bring the men out to the parade grounds here on the sat photo and make them sit on their knees in a straight line. The coup de grace will be shooting these men where they sit. We'll stage a formal execution for that. We want to make sure we get that on video. That will outrage Muslims throughout the world. Now there are a few Egyptian military bases close by so we'll have to be quiet when we execute the raid. Put sound suppressors on your weapons. There can't be any explosions so we'll just have to go into each building and clear it. Sense we'll be leaving the day after tomorrow for Dubai, everyone stay here. I have a van that we can fit in to drive to the airport. Men, this is an important mission. They killed Lola so they will pay dearly for it. I estimate there are around four hundred men at this training camp so it will be a big killing day. Are there any more questions?"

"It sounds like a good plan, Zakkova. We'll be eager to avenge Lola's death so we'll show no mercy to these bastards," said Sammy.

"Ridding the world of these pigs will be all pleasure. Killing Lola was a cowardly act. After we take them out the world will be a safer place," said Doug.

"I will enjoy this mission immensely. We all loved Lola. She was a terrific lady. This will send a message to all those jihadists' pigs that if they kill an innocent person of the United States, we will hunt them down and they will suffer a horrible death," said Mike.

"Okay guys, make yourselves comfortable. We'll go down to the armory now so you can choose your weapons. After that, take them to the firing range and do some practice shooting so you'll feel comfortable with them."

Chapter 32

On the appointed day, the men climbed into the van with their weapons. They were all wearing their black bullet proof combat fatigues and had their special helmets with them. They drove to the airport and boarded Zakkova's Gulfstream. It would take about five hours to get to Dubai. The MC-130H would take off about 1200 hours. That would put them over the Muslim Brotherhood camp at around 0300 hours. The MC-130H was carrying auxiliary fuel tanks so it would not need to stop along the way to refuel nor require aerial refueling.

The men boarded the MC-130H with their HALO packs on schedule. They used the flight time to Egypt to go over the details of the mission again. They were on heightening alert and were psyched out to stage this attack on the Muslim Brotherhood's main training camp. They were all in a killing mode.

When the MC-130H reached its target the loadmaster opened the rear cargo door and the men jumped out of the plane in perfect formation. It was a good HALO jump. They were landing a few yards from each other about a mile from the training camp. They released there parachutes and buried them under some sand. Since they were in a desert terrain, it was flat with no natural barriers. They made their way to the training camp and stopped when they were about three hundred yards from the front gate. There were three guards on duty at the gate. Roger laid down his Barrett Model 821A sniper rifle on the ground and set it on a tripod. Through the special optics on the scope he homed in on his targets and fired three quick rounds. The guard's heads exploded from the force of the high velocity 50 caliber rounds. Now that the front gate was unmanned, the men walked through the gate without any resistance. Sammy took his team to the barracks and the other men fanned out and started killing every Muslim Brotherhood member who was up walking around. There were other guards walking the grounds. The men saw them perfectly with their infrared displays on their helmets. They easily shot down these guards. Once they were sure the grounds were clear of all guards, they entered the buildings to kill anyone in them. There were a lot of men sitting at terminals doing their work. Zakkova's men killed them all and anyone else that was walking around. It took about thirty minutes for the men to kill everyone in the buildings. When they were done, they went back out to the parade grounds. Sammy had fifty men lined up sitting on their knees. These men all came from one of the barracks. They killed all of the men in the other barracks.

"Okay men, stand back about ten yards and aim your weapons at these men. When I give the word fire at the men at will." Many of the Muslim Brotherhood men were crying out for mercy. Most of them were in tears waiting for what they knew their fate was.

"Ready, aim, fire," shouted Zakkova. The men unleashed a fusillade of bullets at the Muslim Brotherhood men. They were all shot to pieces their bodies flinging left and right as the bullets struck them. After the men emptied their clips on the Muslim Brotherhood men, Zakkova went up to each one of them and put a bullet through their heads to make sure all of them were dead.

The men killed over four hundred Muslim Brotherhood members. This would be a major blow to the Muslim Brotherhood. It was doubtful that they could recover from this loss anytime soon.

Zakkova radioed the Ravens and told them they were ready for exfiltration. The Ravens landed just outside of the training camp and the men climbed aboard for their ride back to Dubai where they would fly Zakkova's Gulfstream back to the states.

When they arrived back at Carmel, they all went to Zakkova's house for a debriefing.

"Good job men. This mission was child's play. We took out over four hundred of them with hardly any resistance. We have avenged Lola's death. Let's release the video of the mission this morning. Instead of a voice over we'll do this: We'll start the video with a good picture of Lola and then we'll show the police photograph for her decapitated head. Then we'll show the raid on the training camp ending with the execution of fifty of their men. The video will end with this message "Blood for Blood."

"That's good, Zakkova. That should send a message to all jihadists," said Sammy.

They released the video and the reaction was overwhelming. Muslims throughout the world were rioting in the streets of all major cities. Sheik Yusuf al-Qaradawi, the Muslim Brotherhood's spiritual leader, released a statement condemning the U.S. and Zakkova for this horrendous act. They released a picture of Zakkova and al-Qaradawi offered a $5,000,000 bounty for the jihadist that would bring Zakkova's head to him. The rioters were carrying signs that said "Death to America and Zakkova." Many of the signs had a picture of Zakkova on them.

Egyptian and Interpol authorities were calling the president and the Attorney General demanding that they turn over Zakkova for questioning.

Zakkova flew the men the men back to their homes. When he returned, he packed all of his clothes and all of his weapons and headed back to the airport to his Gulfstream. Zakkova owned an entire island ten miles of the coast of Florida on the gulf side. He had a runway for his Gulfstream there and a house that was a carbon copy of his house in Carmel.

After he arrived at his island, Zakkova received a call on his encrypted satellite phone. It was the president.

"Zakkova, what the hell did you do? I'm getting calls from Egypt and Interpol demanding that I turn you over to them. You created a real shit storm. Muslims are rioting all around the world even in the U.S. We've had to send out the National Guard to quell the violent demonstrations here. It's even worse in Indonesia, Paris and London and all throughout the Middle East," said the president.

"Tell Egypt and Interpol to kiss your ass. You're not about to turn over a highly decorated ex-U.S. Navy SEAL to them. Plus you can truthfully tell them that you don't know where I am. I'm someplace where no one can find me even the NSA. This call has my special encryption software on it so you can't trace it. We left no evidence at the training camp. No one saw us who are still alive. It would be impossible for Egypt or Interpol to prove that I was behind this. Look, the Muslim Brotherhood murdered my fiancé. They decapitated her. Check with Carmel's Sheriff he'll tell you all about it. This was about payback.

"That may be so but in the mind of al-Qaradawi and other jihadists you are already guilty. At least meet with Interpol so they can exonerate you. And I'm very sorry about your fiancé. That is truly tragic. My prayers go out to you and God bless Lola."

"No way can I meet with Interpol. They are infested with Muslim Brotherhood agents. You turn me over to them and no one will ever see me again."

"Okay, I guess you're right about that. But how are we going to stop all of this rioting."

"You need to be tough Mitch. Release a statement that says this attack was perpetrated by a private citizen. That if you even knew where he was you would not turn him over to Egyptian authorities or Interpol. Tell them that the Muslim Brotherhood is to blame for this attack. Tell them that the Muslim Brotherhood came onto our soil and killed an innocent woman and sent thirty-four men on an unsuccessful attack to kill Zakkova Ikanovich. Tell them that the next time they come on our soil and kill an American, that the U.S. government will use all means to track them down and kill them."

"You're right. We can't be perceived as weak on this. That statement will put all terrorists organizations on notice that attacks on our soil against our people will be dealt with harshly. I will do it, Zakkova. What will this do to our little arrangement?"

"I'm too hot to handle. I cannot be seen in D.C. entering the White House. You need to keep your distance from me or you'll have huge political consequences. I am going rogue. I have my target list and Sheik Yusuf al-Qaradawi is at the top of it. I will hunt down and kill leaders of terrorist's organizations, financiers of terrorist's organizations and enablers of terrorist's organizations. Everyone that I kill will be an enemy of the United States."

"I support you 100% on that. We really need you, Zakkova. Is there any way we can still do business together?"

"Yes there is. You can send me missions through my encrypted and untraceable internet connection. We can communicate through that without anyone knowing. This has to be between you and me though. No cabinet members can know what you're doing with me. That bitch Cochran gave every jihadist assassin in the world my picture and my home address. I can't afford to be compromised further. I just don't trust anybody anymore except for General Sherman. I'll need him to supply support for my missions."

"I can do that. I may have to consult General Sherman from time to time to narrow down our targets. My statement you want me to make should shut up Egypt and the Interpol. Once they know that the U.S. is serious about tracking down and killing terrorists they won't want to mess with us."

"I can trust General Sherman so it is alright for you to consult with him."

"Zakkova, I can really feel your pain about Lola and the truth be told, I am ecstatic that you took out the Muslim Brotherhood's main training camp. We have been receiving intel that they were planning an attack on the U.S. in conjunction with al-Qaeda."

"Well, they won't be doing anything for a long time. Taking out four hundred of their top operatives will put a big dent in their operations."

"Yes it will. You've done the country a great service again. I look forward to our continued partnership on the war on terror."

"I am a patriotic citizen and ex-soldier who loves his country. I will always be here to serve you Mitch."

"May God bless you, Zakkova. We need more men of your caliber. I'll be in touch."